TIGER, TIGER

ALSO BY JOHANNA SKIBSRUD

TIGER, TIGER

STORIES

JOHANNA SKIBSRUD

HAMISH HAMILTON
an imprint of Penguin Canada,
a division of Penguin Random House Canada Limited

Canada • USA • UK • Ireland • Australia • New Zealand •
India • South Africa • China

First published 2018

www.penguinrandomhouse.ca

LIBRARY AND ARCHIVES CANADA CATALOGUING IN PUBLICATION

Skibsrud, Johanna, 1980-
[Short stories. Selections]
Tiger, tiger / Johanna Skibsrud.

Short stories.
Issued in print and electronic formats.
ISBN 978-0-7352-3456-7 (paperback).—ISBN 978-0-7352-3457-4 (electronic)

I. Title.

PS8587.K46A6 2018   C813'.54   C2017-904422-2
                                              C2017-904423-0

Cover and interior design by Andrew Roberts

Printed and bound in the United States of America

10 9 8 7 6 5 4 3 2 1

Penguin
Random
House

For John

CONTENTS

TIGER, TIGER

THEY ARRIVED IN PACKING CRATES, like any ordinary shipment—the news delivered to my desk by a breathless Dr. Singh. His thin white hair was askew. It surrounded his face like a halo of light.

"*They've arrived!*" he said, in a voice that—though its tone was a whisper—in register was more like a shout.

We went into the mailroom to have a look. We admired the way the packing tape stretched and shimmered over the seam of each crate, like the smooth surface of burned skin.

Then Günter, our young intern, loaded the crates on a trolley and trundled them into the cramped office I shared with Dr. Wolff. With haste, we cut through the glistening tape and tore through layers of packing fill, to find, nestled toward the bottom, exactly what we were looking for. A small case, roughly the size of my own hand.

I took out the case—was surprised by how light it felt. Even though I hadn't expected it to weigh anything.

I placed it in the middle of my desk, which I had recently cleared, my hand lingering on it a moment as though, if I let it go, it would immediately evaporate into thin air.

Dr. Singh looked at me; he was practically panting with delight. His eyes gleamed over his spectacles, which, as usual, had slipped slightly, down the bridge of his nose. It made you wonder why he wore the glasses at all, the way he strained in order not to look into them.

I can't deny I felt it myself. That same thing, whatever it was, that you could almost see tingling through Dr. Singh's veins. To tell you the truth, I was almost annoyed at Dr. Singh—at the obvious delight he was allowing himself to take in the moment, which for some reason detracted a little from my own. Who can say why, but I suddenly felt an unexpected ripple of disgust at the whole venture. Even though it was as a result of my own efforts—*not* those of Dr. Singh—that we had been presented with the opportunity. And now an enormous responsibility loomed before us.

We bent toward the case on the desk before us, and slowly, very slowly—Dr. Singh at my shoulder—I lifted the lid.

At first, there did not seem to be anything inside at all. We gazed as though into a perfectly empty cylinder. But then, I caught a glimpse . . . not of any *thing* exactly, but of a slight difference in the texture of the case's interior.

It was a thin plastic sleeve, almost as smooth and thin as the packing tape we had removed from the crate's exterior. Identical (I noted, with some surprise), both in quality and dimensions, to an envelope my wife, Franziska, had received last spring from a seed plant in California, after taking it into her head, for some reason, to order away for half a dozen varieties of desert succulents.

It was not long before the seeds arrived. All the way from the United States. How odd, I thought as I held my own thin envelope, that two such very different things, with two very different points of origin—one arriving from the only dimly remembered past, and one from the unforeseeable future—could appear, on the surface at least, almost identical!

And yet what had I expected? What I held in my hand at that moment was just as obscure, just as—nearly—impossible to measure or grasp as that which had already come and gone. Like the past, it did not exist in any conceivable form except as an idea, a wish. A prayer, even! *Here it was* (I felt the fact of it, despite Dr. Singh's form hovering at the corner of my eye, thrill through me): the future itself. No wonder it was nearly invisible to the eye!

With a confidence I did not actually feel, I seized a pair of tweezers from the little tray I kept in the upper left corner of my desk—selecting it from the jumble of more or less useful objects that remained there: thermometers, paper clips, a wind-up airplane given to me on some now long-forgotten occasion by my wife. But the tweezers felt clumsy in my hand, and the distance they introduced between myself and my object only further heightened my sense of remoteness from it. It was disappointing, I thought, and really a bit odd, that this very basic tool—a set of tweezers—was still the best thing so far invented for searching for small items at the bottom of nearly empty bags.

With shame, I realized that my hand had begun to tremble. I redoubled my effort, attempting to clear my mind of every thought—especially as to whether Dr. Singh had noticed the way my hand shook, or that I had begun to perspire.

Finally, I managed to seize on something. I lifted it, tremblingly, from the bag, and Dr. Singh and I crouched together in order to gaze, with wonder and delight, at . . . well, at nothing. We could see almost nothing at all at the tweezers' pinched end. I motioned to Dr. Singh to move aside, and in unison the two of us shuffled a pace or two so that our backs were now to the door rather than to the window, and the specimen was suddenly exposed to the light. Now, we could just barely make out a small speck, as inconsequent seeming as a mote of dust. It was so slightly different in colour and texture from the air that if we had not been looking very hard we would, almost certainly, not have seen it all.

There it was. The tiger.

It had been Dr. Wolff, in fact—not either myself or Dr. Singh—who had stumbled on the idea. He who had first informed us of the team of Russian scientists who had recently unearthed the remains of a laboratory dating back at least a hundred years, since sometime before the Last War. The laboratory had evidently been affiliated with a wildlife sanctuary and had housed the genetic information of at least several now extinct Siberian tigers. The specimens had been carefully stored, and three of them had been recovered—it was tempting to say miraculously—intact. They were now being sold to the highest bidder.

A lab in Moscow had already snatched up one of them, Dr. Wolff informed us. But their science programming hadn't yet fully recuperated from the war, and it was doubtful that anything would come of it. The second specimen had been sold shortly after, to a collector from Brazil. He would keep it on some high shelf in his Rio penthouse, no doubt, Dr. Wolff sniffed. Show it off whenever he remembered it to his more fashionable guests.

The Chinese would almost certainly sweep up the last specimen. Take it back to their laboratories and—hastily, without a thought to the consequences—create their own little monster . . .

"Yes! That would be just like them," Wolff cried. "A scientific approach like that of a spoiled child!"

Dr. Singh began to fiddle with the top button of his laboratory coat. I gazed ahead, using a technique I'd perfected—my eyes making just enough contact with the doctor to suggest attention, but in fact gazing steadily past him, toward the row of high shelves that flanked his desk.

The shelves housed the Wolff's own collection—the extent and variety of which would have impressed even a Brazilian collector. And just like the specimens in Rio, there was no more promising future for these than to remain where they were, gathering dust and waiting for the day when, in a burst of paternal affection, Wolff would take out the feather duster he kept for the purpose and dust each jar—contemplating their secrets, which he alone now kept. His eyes would shine as he dusted the jars in the way that eyes shine only in moments of sincerest love.

How quickly that light would go out once the job was done! It almost made you sorry for him, the way his eyes flickered, then turned inward, toward the trap he had made of his mind. To imagine him in there, shut up and alone—the last of his kind.

Just as for Dr. Wolff, the jars provided me with a source of respite and relief by offering me something to look at while he spoke. For some reason I couldn't bear to listen to him and look at him at the same time. One or the other, yes—but not both. And so I would look behind him at the collection of human and chimp fetuses floating in formaldehyde, their skin grey from long exposure to preserving agents, and think about how strange it was to decay that slowly—or rather, to not decay at all. Because it was the preservative process that was slowly eating away at the specimens, not the other way around—the possibility of their own immortality that was now slowly destroying them. Sometimes I even imagined I could see it happen. That I could actually detect, in the length of time that I gazed at them, their incremental deterioration. (No doubt this was only my imagination; the oldest specimens, boasted Wolff, were nearly four hundred years old. It was quite ridiculous to imagine that given that great length of time I, who was witness only to the smallest fraction of it, might actually be able to *see* the moment in which some identifiable change occurred.)

Other times, I would amuse myself by hazarding guesses at which of Dr. Wolff's specimens were human and which were not, because often in the smaller, less developed specimens it was quite difficult to tell—especially from a distance. I tried to keep my eyes level, and my mind focused on this task, because if I let my eyes drift even slightly—according to some irresistible gravity—down toward the lower shelves, they would inevitably betray me.

The lower shelves housed the doctor's collection of preserved testicles—all of the human variety. It was the second-largest collection of human testicles in the world, Wolff would sometimes boast, transferred into his care by the great-great-grandson of an ex-Nazi surgeon. Wolff maintained the collection "in the name of science," though even he would have had to admit that, by this point, the evidence these specimens supplied was less scientific than spectral; from within their murky jars, they conjured a gruesome past only Wolff was capable of looking in the eye. My own always blinked, compulsively, when they drifted to those lower levels. Or skittered away.

It will be an immense relief, if and when the Wolff ever does finally retire, to clear out those lower shelves. Sometimes I even allow myself the brief fantasy of overseeing the operation. Of course, I would hire someone to do it; I could never bring myself to actually touch them. I would merely watch as the specimens were carried away by a sanitation engineer on a metal dolly, but it would give me a great sense of satisfaction— even pleasure—to see them go.

It wasn't until the following afternoon, after Dr. Wolff had first mentioned the tiger, that Dr. Singh and I, in taking our usual turn together about the laboratory grounds, were able to discuss the matter. Before we had even fallen into step, I knew the direction our conversation would take. I could feel it in the air, a shared idea growing—exerting such an increasing pressure between us that it practically exploded when at last our paths converged.

"Perhaps it is already too late!" Singh exclaimed anxiously, wringing his hands and inserting a peculiar little skip in his step, as he always did when he became especially excited or concerned.

"There is only one way of knowing," I said. My mind had already begun to cool in reflexive response to Singh's agitation. "It is all a question of approach," I said.

"The way the thing might"—skip—"be spun," said Singh.

"That Wolff is opposed to the idea is not entirely to our disadvantage."

"On the contrary, there even seems to be—"

"An increasing interest in ways that the department may—"

"Move forward."

"Who wants to spend their entire career buried in the past?"

"This"—skip—"might really be our chance! It may—"

"Yes. But it will be delicate."

"And yet, at the same time, it might"—skip—"already be too late!"

But it was not too late. Together, Singh and I drafted a letter urging the department to bid on the tiger—and to elect myself as the project head. That was only natural; Singh had spent his career to date working with the genetic material of living organisms, whereas I had always specialized in the dead. My doctoral dissertation had focused on the work of Dr. Alp Tiki, the celebrated Turkish scientist who paved the way for de-extinction back in the last century, with the resurrection of the southern gastric-brooding frog.

The Lazarus Project, as the venture came to be known, also managed to resurrect the dodo, establishing several successful colonies, some of which had even survived the war. However, no one had yet managed, either before or after the war, to introduce the species back into the wild—a fact in support of my own theory, proposed in my dissertation on the subject: the resurrected species had lost its capacity to adapt. The dodo had been reproduced, I had argued, only as a sort of static replica—a "film still," if you will. This was a metaphor I often exploited in the only article I had so far managed to publish, which I had titled, tongue in cheek (a deliberate bid to the popular attention that had briefly been trained on the subject), "Die zweite Auferstehung."

"Is it possible," I had asked, by way of introduction, "to separate genetic material from its historical trajectory? How can any material be 'reproduced' if not within, and as, the very fact of its having, in the first place, arisen?"

The dodo, resurrected by Tiki, existed *outside* of any historical continuum, I explained, and therefore represented the first biological revolution of our common era. The birds were not an ancient genus returned from the dead, but instead an invention of an entirely new species—which one had to acknowledge was, at least in significant part, *human.*

The resurrection of the earth's lost species was not, I argued, an effort that directed us toward a more natural state prior to human intervention, but a way of further propagating the human species in different and multiple forms. It was no doubt for this reason that, while completing my research at Dr. Tiki's sanctuary outside Hamburg, I'd often had the uncanny feeling that all of human history was contained within the glazed, subtly reproachful glare of the dodo. That the eyes who watched me watch them were indeed not the eyes of a bird at all, but the eyes of a human being, and perhaps all human beings, myself included—all of us who had conspired, more or less willingly, not only in the species' initial demise but in its resurrection.

The conclusion of my article was no conclusion at all: "Will our future attempts to study and understand the world around us result only in further demarcating the human being from the rest of the world? Will the human (who so far understands herself primarily in relation to what she is not) cease to exist precisely in the moment—and at the point—where the line separating human beings from other species becomes finally impassable; that is, can be neither imagined nor crossed?"

It would become clear, I reflected (in an earlier version of the article, editorially cut), that no such limit had ever existed at all, that the incarnation of ancient species as essentially human was simply the expression of life—of being itself: its refusal to be bound by any categories at all.

It was my luck that the completion of my dissertation corresponded with a sudden interest in the burgeoning dodo population. A colony had been successfully transported from Dr. Tiki's sanctuary to a Singapore zoo, and for the first time since the war, the public was permitted to view the creatures. The dodo bird became a pop culture sensation. For a few short months the media was wild for it.

Needless to say, it was during this brief period that I had the fortune (or the misfortune, depending on how you looked at it) of publishing my single article. Had it not been for the dodo craze, my small, rather zany paper would probably never have made it past a peer review. In any case, it put a feather in my cap to have my name in print so young, and the piece no doubt contributed to my subsequent hire. But then, of course, shortly after I joined the department—and though the dodo population continued to thrive—interest in their existence fell off dramatically. Almost overnight, I became a dusty academic, the equivalent of a stuffy professor of Latin who continues to insist, despite all evidence to the contrary, on the sustained value and influence of dead languages.

It was for this reason that I now seemed doomed to share an office, in perpetuity, with Dr. Wolff, whose own research was also impossibly out of date. (I had often acerbically suspected that the respect Dr. Wolff still commanded was based on nothing more than his tenacity, the fact that he had now been around "longer than anyone could remember.")

It was really no wonder, when you thought about it, that the dodo had gone so quickly out of fashion. That squat, definitionless body, that dull, nearly expressionless gaze . . . It was impossible not to be consistently reminded of their origin: of the fact that they, more rather than less literally, were a species of the walking dead.

A tiger, on the other hand! There was a figure to capture—and sustain—the imagination. Long enough, at any rate, to publish another article. Perhaps, I considered, I could even manage a whole book before enthusiasm for the idea completely ran its course!

I indulged myself for a moment or two in imagining how I might introduce the topic to future readers: by describing how the idea had first come to me, in the dusty confines of the office "I still shared, at the time," with Dr. Wolff. I would mention the jars: those hundreds of unseeing eyes stacked on the upper and lower shelves—witnesses, all, to the idea as it took shape, and a new life (at once human and more than human) began to stalk its way through the undergrowth of my mind . . .

By the time I got word that the department had approved my application for funding, I had already run the whole project—from its inception to its glorious completion—several times through my mind. Still, it was a surprise to learn that the application had been accepted—and still more of a surprise when, only a week later, I received word from the institute in Moscow that the genetic material of the last Siberian tiger was mine.

I remember I was still in a state of near shock the evening after receiving the news. Franziska had just returned from a conference in Dubai, and when I arrived home from the office she was busy emptying her suitcase, sorting its contents on the bed and folding everything into neat little piles.

I made her sit down. I took her wrists in my hands and sat her down on the bed, disrupting the piles. My heart was beating in my chest like a wild thing that had found itself unexpectedly enclosed.

"What is it?" she asked.

I did not immediately reply. I couldn't. I pressed her wrists toward my chest. I felt a steady pulse beneath my thumb and was unsure if it was hers or mine.

"Come on," she said. Her voice was irritated, or alarmed.

She gave her wrists a shake. I released them.

"The tiger," I said. "The tiger . . . It's mine."

And then, of course, I had to tell her everything from the beginning, starting with Dr. Wolff, because I had not yet breathed a word of it to her, or to anyone—save to the departmental review board and, of course, to Dr. Singh.

For some time, it had actually been quite difficult for me—even under more ordinary circumstances—to speak with

Franziska about my career. We had married during the dodo craze; Franziska was still in graduate school then. There had been no reason to suspect that my career would not continue as promisingly as it had begun.

It wasn't long, however, before I was more than eclipsed. Franziska was now one of the top researchers in the life-extension sciences, and I had yet to publish a single book.

She could hardly have chosen a more fashionable field. While I was staring at the preserved remains of human and animal specimens, and perfecting the art of just-barely-not-listening to Dr. Wolff, Franziska was being courted by just about every major university, science journal, and television network. Her opinion on everything—from the most innovative research being conducted, to the sort of breakfast cereal a person should buy—was sought out and incorporated into advertisement copy and household conversation. Almost every week she had some new engagement: a radio or television interview, a corporate consulting project, an award ceremony, a commencement address.

More often than not she travelled alone, mostly because of the restrictions of my own schedule. This was fine by me. I hated tagging along with her, and she knew it. I couldn't help but withdraw—to feel that whenever I stood at her elbow and someone asked me, "And what do you do?" that it was a form of direct attack. Even, or especially, if they happened to express interest: "Oh, how absolutely fascinating, I never would have thought," or "And how did you choose that particular field?" My skin would prickle and my throat would dry out, so that I would have to reply in short gasps, quickly shutting down the possibility of further communication.

The antagonism I sensed was (as Franziska insisted to me the one time I mentioned it) "all in my head." (Note: I had not intended to mention it at all; it was Franziska who brought it up, chastising me after some function or other for having a "defensive, even combative reaction" to the subject of my work.) "By lashing out," she said, "you *create* the problem you later identify as your reaction's cause, when in fact, you see, it is only an effect."

Perhaps she was right, but that did nothing to change how much I dreaded being caught in a room with her and a throng of other life-extensionists. I could practically hear them wondering to themselves why someone like Franziska had chosen to spend the rest of what would, no doubt, be a very long life with someone like me.

But that was one of Franziska's many charms: her own seeming imperviousness to what other people thought. She had a "fresh outlook," according to the press, a "unique voice"—was even something of a "visionary." In a world devoid of Romance after the devastations of the Last War, she was a romantic. With nothing to return to, she continued to long desperately for a more "natural" course of things.

It was her job not to subvert or alter this course, she maintained, but to attain it more fully—to move closer to, rather than further from, the "essence" of the natural world. It was not all hot air: her more recent scientific studies all convincingly demonstrated that this was indeed possible. That a natural "essence" could in fact be distilled—could be isolated and removed from such chance outcomes as disease and old age.

Her announcement (casually, last spring, in the course of a

television interview) that she was considering naturally conceiving, and bearing, a child, should not have come as a shock to anyone who had been closely following the trends in Franziska's career. It was in line with both her romantic impulses and her predilection for all things "organic"—yet she surprised everyone. No one, perhaps, more than me.

In recent years, the life-extension sciences had made childbearing virtually obsolete. If—as it now appeared, thanks to Franziska's own dedicated research on the subject—human beings had the capacity to live as good as forever, we quite simply didn't have the resources to support any future generations. Not, at any rate, until the food science and space travel industries had been given the opportunity to catch up.

According to the press, Franziska's desire to have a child was something she "felt deeply"—something she really "couldn't explain"—but the first time I'd heard anything about it was by watching the six o'clock news. Because of this, I couldn't help but suspect, in less generous moods, that Franziska had first taken an interest in the idea more or less as a publicity stunt.

Perhaps she had been inspired by the genetics professor we had shared in our university days (it was in his class that Franziska and I had, in fact, first met), who had augmented his reputation in the field with the idiosyncratic detail, known to everyone, that he was the adoptive father of twelve. How could a *life-extensionist* like Dr. Franziska Scheller (everyone, as she well knew, was bound to wonder) bat away the threat of extreme overpopulation her chosen field of science had virtually invented, with the mention only of a "deep desire" she couldn't otherwise explain?

I should have guessed, of course. Long before Franziska's announcement on the six o'clock news. Franziska later said so herself—as if the misunderstanding between us had somehow been my fault. If I had been "paying attention," she said . . .

And it was true. I might certainly have noticed that for nearly a year, no matter where she was in the world, Franziska had flown back each month for at least a twenty-four-hour period— during which time I was placed under the most direct of pressures to perform the necessary function of my sex.

After long absences, these pressures were—at first, at least— most welcome. But after Franziska made her announcement, her urgency to conceive a child increased dramatically. So abrupt and so direct was the pressure I was now under that I often found myself quite unable to perform.

This drove Franziska nearly mad with distraction. What was I was afraid of? she asked. Did I not truly love her? Want her to bear my child? Did I think it was wrong? Was my reaction (or rather, my lack of any reaction at all) a judgment, in whole or in part, on her and her desires?

Again and again, I promised her, on all counts yes, when it was appropriate to do so, and on all counts no, when that was instead the answer required. And indeed, though my initial reaction to Franziska's announcement had been one of skepticism and surprise, it was not long before I, too, began to feel something I "couldn't explain": a feeling that, once detected, I realized must always have existed—but so "deeply" within me, I had never suspected it was there. And so, on most occasions it was not on account of either fear or reluctance (as Franziska suspected) but on account of my own almost unbearable desire that I—quite literally—shrank from my task.

You can only imagine Franziska's disappointment, after having taken a red-eye flight from Auckland or New York or Shanghai. And though, in the end, we always somehow managed, they were nights I would rather forget.

And still—after months, now, of the most concentrated efforts on both our parts, we were no closer to achieving our goal. This placed our personal relationship under considerable strain. Rather than resulting in any direct conflict between us, however, it diluted something. We became abstract; each to the other only half the idea we were attempting to express.

But what was that idea? It was a question that, though it remained unspoken, charged every thought or remark that passed between us. Even the most ordinary statements seemed to end on an elevated note.

It was becoming evident that, contrary to what we had always thought, there was, between us, nothing "essential"— that our relationship was the result of nothing more than dumb chance.

There was a time when we would have exalted in this. In the pure "luck" (we had called it then) of our having met one another at all. In the inessential details of behaviour and form that had—by first capturing our attentions—led us near blindly into love. I had been struck, for example (almost literally; I remember the sensation, like being pulled under by a sudden wave), with the way that Franziska adjusted her eyeglasses when momentarily disconcerted or confused, by the small dimple that appeared in the high upper left corner of her cheek when she smiled. It was impossible to guess what litany of gratuitous details had first inspired Franziska to notice me, but they had existed. Despite her personal and professional proclivity for the "essential" and the "absolute," there is no doubt that, at the beginning, she had as little a grasp of my "essence" as I had of hers.

What was now becoming clear was that, even after the many years we had spent with one another, we had moved no closer toward an understanding.

Testament to this was Franziska's reaction when I mentioned the tiger.

"But have you considered the thing fully?" She had risen from the bed and had turned her attention back to her disrupted piles.

My hands, which had been raised, dropped to my knees.

Considered the thing fully . . . I ran the words a second time through my mind. Did she realize how preposterous they sounded? How absolutely counter to science? How on earth, I wondered— exasperated—could one *fully consider* what did not yet exist? What was only an idea, a matrix of possible circumstances, arisen from a previous matrix of possible circumstances?

And how could Franziska, who knew this (and who knew, too, that this was the first genuine opportunity I had so far been granted in my entire career), respond in this way? What was required was not *consideration*, I reflected anxiously, but a simple decision: was one, or was one not, willing or able to take what, even in the most scientific terms, could be called nothing other than "a leap of faith"?

Yes! I was willing! Of course I was! I could feel it—my own willingness—trembling inside me, like a plucked wire.

But instead of explaining this to Franziska, I said only: "Of course I have!"

My voice was harder than I had expected it to be.

"Excuse me," Franziska said, and tugged at the sleeve of a button-down shirt, which I had pinned beneath my knee.

I got up quickly and the shirt flew toward her, unfolding itself and waving like a flag at the end of her hand.

"I mean," I implored her—the sudden panic in my voice accelerating rather than softening my tone—"what is there to consider? We are faced with . . . a prospect, a genuine opportunity. I should instead be asking you, have you considered the matter? I mean, truly. Have you tried, even for a moment, to grasp what this means? What it could begin to mean . . . for me personally, yes, but also for the future of science? Of history? Of the world—not as we know it, but as we might one day begin to imagine it to be?"

Franziska was silent. Carefully, painstakingly, she folded the shirt and placed it on the bed.

"And what about for him—or her," she said, very quietly. "For the tiger. Have you considered it from her perspective? You've told me yourself," she continued, carefully, "how unique the tiger is among mammals, how curiously human their emotional responses have been observed to be. That they can feel genuine rage, sorrow. Have, if threatened, been known to take elaborate, performative, revenge. Have you considered how this emotional capacity might develop, or express itself, in a specimen like the one you describe—one that's been cut off from even the possibility of contact and communication with its own species, from the very idea of history, and, therefore, from any sense of what it even means to be a tiger? It strikes me," she concluded, "not so much as a question for science but as a moral dilemma!"

Now I was genuinely annoyed. "Oh, morality!" I said. "Nice of you to mention it. Need I remind you that I've been turning this question over for my entire career? That the moral dilemma to which you refer is the very basis of any study of the deep past, and of the possible future—the two regions to which my field of research is particularly and devotedly bound? While you"—I took a deep breath—"you and your esteemed colleagues have been busy extending our lives beyond all reasonable limits at the expense of countless future generations whom you have barely paused to consider, I," I said, "have been moving at a snail's pace, floundering in semi-darkness, searching for any possible foothold . . . Do you remember my dissertation?" I asked. "The complex argument I developed, the questions I broached—specifically against the advice of my advisory committee, who warned me not to get 'in too deep'? Do you remember 'Die zweite Auferstehung' in Progressiv Biologie Heute?" I took another deep breath. "Do you remember the dodos?"

Franziska stared at me, her face blank. She appeared suddenly tired and—the thought surprised me, but once it had been thought I could not un-think it—old. Not in any physical sense, of course. Not to be vigilant about something like that would not be "eccentric" in Franziska's line of work; it would be career suicide. There were no lines or wrinkles around her eyes, and her body was as slim and lithe as it had always been; her hair

was as sleek, her skin as fresh and as smooth as on the first
day we met. But there was something new . . . something . . .
Then it hit me. I had perceived—distinctly, and in that exact
moment—a genuine change. In Franziska, or in my relationship toward her. A change that, though it had no doubt taken
place slowly, over time—though it had in this sense *always* been
occurring—had also occurred in precisely that moment. And I
had witnessed it.

But that I had witnessed it . . . did this not suggest that a change
had occurred in me as well? That I, too, had—over the time
Franziska and I had known one another—grown old?

The idea did not frighten me. Instead, I felt a sudden, distinct
pleasure at the thought. Even—yes, arousal. Something stirred
in me. I approached Franziska. I extended my hand toward her
and touched her cheek—the exact place where, if she smiled, a
dimple would suddenly appear.

She was not smiling now. Nonetheless I knew exactly where
the dimple would be, and touched it.

Did she soften—even slightly—at my touch?

I let my hand fall gently, so that my palm cupped her cheek.
At first she did not respond at all, but then, slowly, very slowly,
she relaxed the muscles of her neck and allowed me to support
the weight of her head and neck in my hand.

Then, very suddenly, she drew back. "I'm sorry," she said.
"I'm—very tired." She returned to her task.

Perhaps I should not have reacted so fiercely. The "moral"
question had become particularly charged between us of late,
and I knew very well she was still feeling sensitive. It had come
up when, only a few weeks before, we read together the findings

of a new study conducted by a team of geneticists (one of them none other than our own former professor) about the discovery of a "moral code" within the basic structure of human DNA. The research team concluded that one was either born with the "moral gene" or one was not. An argument had almost immediately erupted between Franziska and me, which, rather than being resolved, had merely petered out into a short exchange of such statements as "Well that's your opinion then," and "I suppose I'm not going to change your mind."

Franziska—immediately dismissive of the report—had argued vigorously that the "so-called" code reflected nothing more about human morality than the biases of those who'd detected it.

"But why," I remember countering (I was genuinely curious), "is the idea so distasteful to you, so difficult to imagine? You! Who have devoted yourself to unlocking the very *essence of life!*"

"Precisely for that reason!" Franziska had returned. "Because I have come to understand enough about the *essence of life* to know that it can't be reduced, the way this research proposes it does, and that no single part of it exists in isolation!"

"A flimsy evasion!" I shot back. "Are you suddenly a poet?"

She threw up her hands. "And yet, if we accept this," she said, "if we concede our capacity for 'moral' judgment on the basis of something invisible to the eye—the existence of which we must merely take on faith—what separates us from the cultivated ignorances, and blindnesses, of our most unguided ancestors?"

"Well, what is the alternative?" I shouted. "Shall we repress science? Turn things over to the masses? Have some fanatic— some semi-educated boob—draw up a chart, willy-nilly, one column for 'right' and one for 'wrong'? Why should we continue to trust and accept the inexplicable and conflicting impulses according to which human history has so far been driven, if there exists—as this research suggests there does—another, better, and more obvious way?"

And then it occurred to me—just a glimmer of an idea, which I tried immediately to put from my mind. Was it possible, I wondered, that Franziska was herself deficient of the "moral gene"? Was it not likely that a primary indication that one lacked the "moral gene" was a failure to accept the possibility of its existence? A willingness to accept—even an enthusiasm for—ambiguity?

A chill shivered through me. Perhaps to pursue childbirth with Franziska was, after all, rather ill advised? Who knew what hidden predilections, what invisible gaps or shortcomings, we might unknowingly pass on to our children, given that we had not yet had the chance to fully discover them within ourselves?

I thought perhaps I would press Franziska, despite her romantic ideas on the subject (how badly she had wanted to "throw herself" into the thing! To just let it "happen"), toward having ourselves thoroughly examined by that geneticist, our former professor, who might subsequently warn us of any gene (or lack thereof) that could prove disadvantageous to a potential, future child. It had by this point become quite obvious, after all, that if "it" was going to happen, it was not going to be "naturally." Yes, I considered, we had a responsibility to make as certain as possible that . . .

But just as quickly as the thought occurred, I stamped it out. No doubt this, too, was a defensive gesture. It would be impossible, I realized in the split second after the thought had occurred, to go on living life with Franziska—perhaps to go on living at all—if I was to believe her lacking in this crucial, one might even say essential, way. Coolly, deliberately, I pushed the thought into the darkest corners of mind.

It did not always stay there, of course. As usual, once conceived, the idea had a life of its own and there was really no telling when or along what pathways it would come—but when it did come, it came as an irrelevant flash, which, for the most part, did not even merit the distinction of being called a "thought."

But here it was again, weeks later, as I watched Franziska calmly, fiercely, sweep her empty suitcase from the bed. Well, really, I thought, as she disappeared into the closet. It might explain a few things. But then she reappeared, turned toward me, and adjusted her glasses in the way she always did when she became in any way disconcerted or confused.

"Well, I'm glad," she said. "I can only imagine how very exciting this must be." Then she burst into tears.

There was no way I could have anticipated it. Franziska was romantic, yes, but she had never been overt, exactly, with her emotions, and was certainly not prone to tears. In fact, the more upset she became, the more she steeled herself against them. Her edges became harder, more distinct; I could sometimes almost feel them in the air between us. They had, for example, pressed in upon me sharply—had nearly taken my breath away—on those terrible evenings after she had flown the red-eye from Auckland or New York and the two of us had lain, angry and disappointed, in one another's arms. ("Is it me?" she had asked.

"My body?" Impossible; that perfect body, upon which it would be unreasonable to expect anyone—who did not attend very carefully, over a very long period of time—to detect any discernible change. "Do you not love me?" Equally impossible: often, and despite everything, when I looked at her, I still felt that same sense of going under, of being swallowed by a sudden wave. "Are you afraid?" Here I would have no choice but to hesitate, but increasingly I could reply with some confidence, "No.") But despite how she tortured herself—and me—on those occasions, she had never once cried. And now here she was: her face crumpled, her back hunched as though she had been hit, her hands dropped helplessly to her sides—suddenly racked with sobs.

"What is it?" I asked. I rushed toward her—"What is it? What is it?"—before I was even quite certain why, or what I would do when I reached her. "What is it? What is it?"

My arms closed around her. She did not pull away. But she did not stop crying either. There was nothing more I could do, I realized, but hang on. So I did, and Franziska cried until she couldn't any longer and her sobs gave way to rasping sighs.

"Shh . . . shh . . ." I whispered. "It's all right, it's all right . . ."

That was six months ago now. Franziska recovered; apologized. The incident had not been mentioned again. I am not sure, therefore, why exactly it came to mind in the moment that, crouched next to Dr. Singh, and squinting into the light, I first glimpsed the nearly invisible germ of a long-extinct tiger at the end of the pinched tweezers I held, tremblingly, in hand. I gazed at that beautiful, monstrous thing, and I thought of the way my arms had opened, extended themselves, had—without thinking—closed around Franziska. As though that would be enough. How the words I had used had tumbled from me, unbidden—emerging from somewhere deep inside me. As though there was a place in me that actually believed, not just in the idea but in the actual physical presence within the body of that most invisible and most improbable thing, which I have so far been able to define with no greater accuracy than that common and most rudimentary of terms: "love."

KEY LIME,
1994

HERO COULD QUITE HONESTLY SAY she hadn't felt this way for several decades. Seriously. Not since she was a teenager on forced road trips with her parents back and forth from Spokane to Eugene to visit her sister, Zoe—already in college by then. For seven straight hours, her parents would sit in the front seat and argue, and Hero, with her headphones on, would sit in the back and pretend that she didn't exist.

Yes, quite honestly, she could say that was the closest she had ever come to genuine despair. Even after her divorce, which had been messy as hell, she had merely oscillated between vengeful euphoria and a state of trance-like acceptance, adopting a sort of banal fatalism and embarrassing herself, both in public and private, by saying things like "Things always happen for a reason" and "It's probably for the best." These and other inanities she later blamed on never, during that entire period, having gotten a full night's sleep (Quinn had still been a toddler then). But she'd been lucky, too; had been able to afford a certain amount of hackneyed fatalism—to be gloriously, rather than desperately, vengeful. Rog had left her the same week her first solo show had received a glowing review in the *L.A. Times*. It had been the first and, frankly, so far the only exciting moment of her artistic career.

———

Stepping out of the climate-controlled car into the midday heat was like stepping into a brick wall. She was reminded again of road trips with her parents: how her father would pull off angrily at historical markers (she was quite certain then, as now, that he did it not to satisfy any personal interest but out of pure spite). He would turn to her in the back seat and, with exaggerated courtesy, inquire if she thought she might be able to drag herself from the car. He had no idea it was a literal request. Hero's legs—when she did somehow manage to follow her father to the curb—felt, beneath her, as though they'd been made out of lead.

Hero felt something like this now, and couldn't explain why. She'd been coming to the Paradise Valley Senior Center to visit her grandmother, Kitty Moy, every Tuesday afternoon for the past fifteen years—as long as Quinn had been alive. If she didn't exactly look forward to her visits, she had certainly never dreaded them. She considered it a duty, and was proud—even perhaps a little smug—about the fact that she rarely missed a week.

Even after, as Kitty deteriorated, it hardly mattered anymore. Over the last year or so it had become increasingly apparent that Kitty's short-term memory was pretty well shot: she could hold on to new information for periods of only about fifteen minutes. Hero could have come six times a week or not at all and it would have been, to Kitty, more or less the same. But still, continuing her regular visits was important to Hero, even if (at least in any obvious way) it was no longer important to Kitty.

The visits had, after all, been the one consistent thing in her life since Quinn was born. And besides, no one else was going. Her parents still lived in Spokane and hardly travelled anymore.

Zoe, even if she had lived nearby, would never have been able to "take the time" (she was an announcer on the Channel 10 news out of San Diego. The way she talked about it, it seemed she honestly believed that nothing would actually happen if she wasn't there at six every evening to announce that it had). Ordinarily, just the fact that out of everyone in her family it was she alone who had made any sort of effort was enough for Hero to feel personally gratified. As if her "good works" could really serve to counterbalance the criticisms (mostly unspoken, and predominantly imaginary) aimed at her from both Zoe and her parents.

From Zoe: the concern that she had never remarried, and didn't even have a proper boyfriend; that she had never managed to make something of herself. (Aside from that single solo show the year Rog left, she'd never again been mentioned in the L.A. Times.)

From her parents, the reproaches all revolved around Quinn. From the beginning, Hero and Rog had been meticulous about splitting both time and parental duties as near as possible down the middle—and for just as long, Hero's parents had silently warned her that all that was really being compromised was their son.

To think that she might have offset these and other concerns with a weekly visit to Kitty Moy was, of course, absurd; it was precisely because of the choices both Zoe and her parents held in such contempt that Hero had been able to maintain, if nothing else over the past fifteen years, her regular Tuesday afternoon visits.

So, all right. There was no way around it. It was not Kitty who needed Hero, but the other way around. Perhaps especially this fall after Quinn had informed her he'd prefer to live full-time with Rog. Just like that. Out of the blue. As she was driving him to the arts magnet school out in Pasadena he'd just begun attending this year.

"It'll be easier for all of us," he'd told her. She could practically hear how the words had being rehearsed ahead of time. They certainly weren't his. But they didn't sound like Rog either; Rog would never have thought to use the first person plural— even in the form of a patronizing cliché.

No doubt she had the new school counsellor, Devon, to thank. An irritating young man who gave Hero the uncanny feeling whenever he spoke to her that she was a character in one of his "case study" scenario flash cards.

But Quinn seemed to like him.

"What about school?" Hero had asked after he'd made his announcement. It was the only thing she could bring herself to say out loud.

Quinn was silent. Which meant, evidently, that it went without saying for all of them—Quinn, Rog, and even the sympathetic Devon—that she would continue to shuttle Quinn to and from school, nearly an hour each way in the worst traffic, though now *none* of the days would be officially "hers." "Her" time would now amount to just that: the roughly two hours she and her son would spend stuck in traffic, driving back and forth between Pasadena and Venice Beach.

Because, of course, she *would* continue to drive him. It did go without saying, because it *also* went without saying that Rog was, and always would be, off the hook. That his other commitments were just far more important than hers—demanding in ways that neither she nor Quinn could be expected to understand.

Possibly, this was true. If only because Hero had never managed to settle into a genuine "career" (i.e., a way of earning a
steady income) the way Rog had. He'd worked his way up to
general manager of a large pool company, and last year had been
able to buy up a sizeable share. She was meanwhile working part-
time at an early learning centre called Journeys, where she taught
"aesthetic and creative development" to three-year-olds. The best
part was that it was flexible. The director didn't mind if she
arrived late or had to cancel suddenly because of a schedule glitch
with Quinn. No one, not even Journeys parents, became overly
concerned if three-year-olds missed out on a few minutes, here
or there, of their "aesthetic and creative development."

Who knew, though, really, the sort of long-lasting effects
those missed minutes had on a child? Hero had thought this
angrily from time to time—though never really in earnest.
Perhaps, she'd reflected (half to punish Rog and half to punish
herself), they were just as important, or more so, than getting
a design delivered, or following up on a shipment complaint.

Inside Paradise Valley it was cool. The girl at the desk looked up,
smiled blandly, and indicated the guestbook with the stamen
end of a synthetic flower taped to the side of her pen. Hero
signed her name in the book, then checked the time and
scratched it into the adjacent box: 1:34. She was always extremely
precise when she wrote in both the "time in" and "time out"
columns.

She started toward her grandmother's room, but had not
gone far when she met one of the nurses, Gina, coming in the

opposite direction. Gina had a full tray of meds and they rattled as she approached. "Oh, honey," she said, "the wedding got moved back. The bride's late again, I'm afraid. They're all still in the auditorium."

Before Hero had an opportunity to ask, "What wedding?" Gina waved for her to follow. "I'll take you," she said, without looking over her shoulder. Her career had cultivated in her a brisk, practical manner that so seamlessly integrated graciousness and command that it was impossible to tell if you were being taken care of or ordered about.

Hero double-stepped to catch up.

"What wedding?" she asked. She said it as though she was trying to recall something she'd forgotten—but there was nothing to recall.

Gina just nodded. "That's right," she said. "It got moved from Thursday to Tuesday this week because of the bride's schedule—but look, now she's late again anyway. Honestly. We all love her, but if it keeps up, we're going to have to get a different bride."

At first it had been just the occasional slip-up. Difficulty retrieving a name, a misplaced detail in a story. Small blunders that could be masked almost successfully by Kitty's habit of speaking irreverently, jumping from subject to subject, trailing off mid-sentence, referring to even her closest friends as "what's her name . . ." But then the larger moorings began to go. She would forget the day, the time of year, where she was, who was still alive, who wasn't, and why. Once the details had been reintroduced, she would do all right for a while, but then a few minutes later she'd be adrift again.

It had been Hero's idea to set up a large whiteboard across from Kitty's favourite chair onto which the morning nurse wrote down the date, the weather, and any important event that might be happening that day. When Hero came, she wrote down something about her own life. Just some little thing that would serve to remind Kitty over the course of the week, whenever she looked up, that Hero had been for her Tuesday visit—and would come again. Last week, for example, Hero had written "Quinn is enjoying his first weeks at school," even though she didn't quite know if it was true. During the nearly two hours they spend together every day in the car, she and Quinn barely speak. They listen in reverential silence (enforced by Quinn) to Quinn's iPhone, set to shuffle. Even though the playlist is therefore allegedly random, Hero can never tell one song, let alone one band, from the other because they all sound the same. A dispassionate lyrical whine: the very sound, she once complained to Zoe, of repression. "I honestly find myself hoping," she'd said, "he'll suddenly develop an interest in thrash punk, or death metal." She would turn the volume up herself, she promised. Until the car shook and people turned to stare at them when they stopped at the lights. A few good death metal albums would, she quipped, be a hell of a lot cheaper than therapy.

At first Hero had thought: a couple of the residents, probably. It did happen from time to time. Since Hero had been visiting Paradise Valley, there had been four or five weddings, one memorable divorce. It was supposed to be heartwarming. And it was. It reassured you: "It's never too late!" But what Gina had said about needing "a new bride" threw her. She must have looked as confused as she felt, because Gina laughed. "You've been coming here how long and you've never been to a wedding?" she asked. "We've been doing them—what?—two, three years? Every week! Same place—" She threw her head back and rolled her eyes exaggeratedly. "*Usually* same time. You'll see. They just love them. Kitty especially. Cries like a baby."

They had reached the metal doors that led to the building's central auditorium. At other times, card games were held here, the occasional movie was shown. Gina pulled one of the doors open partway so that Hero could peer inside. The tables had been pushed against the walls and plastic chairs were set up in rows. About twenty or twenty-five resident "guests" were seated, mostly in groups of twos or threes. They filled roughly half of the available chairs. At the front of the room was a low stage, where—behind a pressboard table evidently serving as an altar—the celebrant rocked patiently from heel to toe, in a slow, rhythmic motion. He was wearing a bright red button-down shirt, tinted prescription glasses, and orthopaedic sneakers.

The groom stood to his immediate left, arms dangling awkwardly. He was twenty-five roughly, of medium height and weight, and vaguely familiar to Hero, though she couldn't say why. His suit didn't fit properly; the shoulders of the jacket were too broad and the pants were too long, slouching over a pair of scuffed-up black trainers.

"Pomp and Circumstance" was being piped in through the small speakers at the back of the room. There were white streamers and a few vases of plastic flowers at the head of the stage.

Hero checked her watch: 1:43. And the ceremony hadn't even started yet. Usually she stayed only about half an hour. Sometimes less—twenty minutes or so. Hero would ask Kitty how she was feeling and then sit there nodding—periodically contributing a small, sympathetic exhale—while Kitty rattled off a list of her latest complaints.

Even before her memory had begun to go, it was rare that Kitty asked a single question.

Then the two of them would watch Zoe on TV together and about midway through Hero would announce that she regretted she couldn't stay longer. She'd give Kitty's hand a squeeze, a quick peck on the cheek, then leave her to watch the next six broadcasts of the six o'clock news. All the rooms at Paradise Valley were hooked up to cable, and Kitty could have watched Zoe on Channel 10 any day of the week at the regular time, but, of course, she always forgot. Last Christmas, Hero had bought her a slow-mo subscription, and they now recorded all of Zoe's broadcasts. When she came on Tuesday afternoons, Hero queued the system so that after watching the previous Tuesday's broadcast together, Kitty could watch the rest of the week's broadcasts in a single go. And she did watch—positively rapt. Exclaiming all the while in delight over Zoe's hair and makeup. Even when she momentarily forgot who Zoe was, it didn't seem to matter. Hero had wryly reported as much to Zoe on more than one occasion. "Space and time simply melt away," she had said. "You transcend."

The few times that Hero had stayed with Kitty long enough to watch more than one broadcast, she had found it unsettling.

The democratic sincerity of Zoe's voice so significantly undercut the distance between reported events that, before too long, Hero found she could no longer distinguish between them. A story about a woman driving off a bridge into the San Luis Rey River, for example, and a story about early voter registration struck her as disconcertingly parallel.

Adding to the confusion was Kitty. She would beam at the television from across the room, periodically exclaiming, "What a pretty girl! What a *very pretty girl!*"

"Go on," Gina said. She indicated Kitty, who was seated alone, about midway down a central aisle. She was wearing a turquoise pantsuit with a tricoloured pastel scarf, her signature bouffant dyed an iridescent blue. Hero made her way down Kitty's mostly empty row. She hunched her shoulders a little, apologetically, as if that might make her appear smaller. At the front of the room, the celebrant was still shifting patiently from foot to foot and the groom—whom she now recognized as one of the attendants—stood by as if awaiting final judgment.

Yes, of course—that was it, Hero thought. She had often seen him pushing the residents to and from the cafeteria, his face set in exactly the same mixture of resignation and dismay.

Hero touched Kitty's shoulder and Kitty turned, beamed. "Sweetheart!" She took up Hero's hand and gave it a firm squeeze. "You *made it!*" she said. "I'm so glad."

Long before her memory went, it had been one of Kitty's strategies to be extravagant and impartial with affection. On the one hand, it guaranteed that she didn't offend anyone who presumed themselves of some importance, and on the other, it flattered those who didn't.

Hero sat down, feeling irritated. Again, she looked at her watch: 1:46. Okay, she told herself. I'll give it till two. She was usually out the door by two anyway. Or shortly after. She looked toward the double doors at the back of the auditorium, where presumably the bride would shortly be arriving. Then back toward the front.

Really, she should just slip out now. Leave a note on the whiteboard: "Nice to see you, Grandma!"

What more, on any other occasion, did her visits amount to?

It was, for some reason, the doily covering the pressboard altar toward which she now found her attention drawn. What a truly preposterous object, she thought. And yet, she could clearly recognize within it (perhaps, indeed, it was the very origin of) her own "aesthetic and creative development."

She remembered how, on the few occasions she'd visited Kitty in Hancock Park as a child, she'd followed her grandmother about—lingering over the polished china figurines on the mantelpiece, which, once or twice, she'd even been permitted to lift, briefly, in her hands. She remembered how absolutely transported she had been by their shimmering forms. Life was not a series of objects, they seemed to suggest, but of possibilities, of angle and light!

Yes, it was from Kitty—with her spoon collection, her doilies, her candelabras and porcelain figurines—that Hero had first learned about beauty. Her mother had always emphatically avoided the word, but Kitty used it all the time. A painting or a flower was beautiful—but so was a sweater, or a chicken sandwich.

Hero, too, had been beautiful. She remembered the distinct pleasure she used to feel when Kitty drawled out a compliment to Hero's long legs or fine hair. It was a vexed pleasure, because of the way that her mother always stiffened in reaction to the word, but it was a pleasure nonetheless.

In their own household—the drab log home her father had built for them outside Spokane, with its serviceable little kitchen garden—the word "beauty" referred only to museum art, symphonic music, or things that happened to people in books. In her grandmother's house, beauty was a thing you could touch. It was crocheted doilies and glass lamps. It was long hair, lean calves, air conditioning, and the scent of Nuits de Paris.

The door at the back of the room screeched open, and two overweight girls in peach-coloured dresses came marching slowly down the aisle. Nurses, or nurse's aides, Hero thought. But she didn't recognize them.

Kitty patted Hero's hand as they passed, then turned, craning her neck to watch the door.

At LACMA right now, there was this James Turrell retrospective going on.

Hero had gone last week with her friend Anjali. "It used to be like this," Hero had said, gazing at a projection of a fluorescent square on the wall. "Art was everywhere, wasn't it? It used to be enough to say—look."

Anjali had twisted her mouth into a knot and nodded. The two of them sat down on a bench opposite the projected square.

It was difficult to know when to stop looking.

It used to be, Hero considered, as she followed Anjali into the next room, that a limit was a suggestion, an invitation. Nowadays, it was just a limit. It was a raised eyebrow, a shrug. Quotation marks hovering like a set of claws around any idea made vulnerable by hesitating too long in the air.

In the hologram room, she passed her hand through each of the images.

It is not an illusion, she thought. She could see it quite clearly: the way her hands *actually disrupted* something.

By the time she looked up, Anjali had moved on, and that was why, several minutes later, she ended up wandering alone into "Key Lime, 1994."

The room was so dark that upon first entering, Hero had to walk with her hands stretched straight out in front of her so she wouldn't bump into anything. She could make out a dozen or so shadows—people moving through a green light at the centre of the room. Compelled, she continued walking toward the light and the light got brighter and brighter until, stepping past a gauzy dividing curtain, she was confronted with a near-blinding fluorescent glare and a tangle of exposed wires.

She stood there, stunned. So, not even light escapes, she thought. Even light becomes a limit, a trope, a convention . . .

But then a guard barked out, "Oh no! *Excuse* me! You can't go in there!"

Obediently, Hero stepped out of the light. Now, of course, the darkness was not as dark as it had seemed. The people did not appear to her as shadows but as distinct individuals: a few college students, an older gay couple consulting the museum brochure, a woman wearing a baby on her back in a sling.

The guard was still moving toward her, her hands outstretched in alarm, but also, no doubt, because—having just re-entered the room—she could barely see.

"I'm very sorry," the guard said, as she reassumed her post at the limit of the artwork—a limit marked (it had by now become clear) by the thin gauze curtain Hero had unthinkingly stepped through just a moment before. "You're just really not supposed to go in there." She seemed more embarrassed than angry, now, though. How, after all, was anyone to know—without the presence of the guard—where the piece ended or began?

Now the bare fluorescent bulb, still glaring at them from the other side of the curtain—the same bulb that had struck her as a sad testament to the demise of art in the twenty-first century, an apocalyptic drive toward the dead centre of things—seemed to Hero, instead, like a revelation. All that input and output! That obscene brightness! That confusion of sockets and wires!

At last, the bride appeared, framed in the doorway. Pretty. A big, open face, wide lips. Something keen—expectant—about her. The dress was all right, too. Pretty classic. Off-white. Lace at the neckline and at the arms, a medium train that dragged audibly on the auditorium's parquet floor.

The groom's eyes still wandered, but the bride's were steady, and she took her time getting down the aisle. The way that she held herself—self-possessed almost to the point of shyness— made it seem as though whatever she was approaching had nothing whatsoever to do with the humiliated groom, the piped-in music, the pressboard altar, the plastic chairs . . . Instead of wishing for everything to hurry along, Hero found herself willing the bride to check her pace. How slowly, she wondered, was it technically possible to progress down the aisle? Was it possible for the bride to proceed so slowly—so deliberately— that it would take virtually forever for her to actually arrive? Was it possible that, after a certain point, her progress might even begin to reverse itself? That she might begin to be blown, instead, back up the length of the aisle toward the metal doors at the back of the room? Back, still further: out into the hall, the parking lot, and finally back along whatever complicated free- way system she had come?

But, no. Despite Hero's best efforts, the bride only continued to move steadily forward. At last, she reached the stage and stepped onto it, carefully. The groom offered her his hand, she took it. The celebrant began his address.

"We are gathered today . . ."

Beside her, Kitty fumbled in her purse.

Hero wondered if the bride and groom had known each other before they started getting married every week.

Finally, from her purse's depths, Kitty managed to retrieve a Kleenex and now she patted with it at the corner of her eyes and nose.

"Do you, Jason Stanley Ruiz," the celebrant continued, "take this woman, Alison Nicole Howe . . ."

If they used their real names . . .

The tears had begun to flow freely down Kitty's face. She no longer attempted to wipe them away.

They hadn't, Hero noted, changed the "love, honour, and obey" part to "love and cherish."

A quick peck on the lips; perhaps a genuine blush from the groom. Funny how weeks' worth of practice had not made a public kiss any less clumsy, or embarrassing.

Kitty blew her nose loudly. Then the first notes of "Ode to Joy" sounded and the couple marched together up the aisle.

"Beautiful," Kitty murmured as they walked together back to Kitty's room. "Just beautiful."

But by the time they arrived, the wedding was forgotten. Kitty settled into her favourite chair, and Hero scrolled back through a week's worth of Channel 10 news broadcasts, then pressed Play. Zoe's face, open-mouthed—frozen mid-sentence in a sort of Munch-like scream—reassumed its customary proportions. The steady rhythms of her voice suggested a comforting equivalence between the extraordinary and the mundane. Hero crossed the room to the whiteboard and picked up the dry-erase pen attached to the corner of the board by a string.

She couldn't think what to write.

A university in Texas was in lockdown after an attempted shooting earlier that morning, announced Zoe. El Chapo's pilot had been caught and arrested somewhere.

Hero snapped the lid off the pen. "Quinn enjoying his first weeks at school!" she wrote. The point was not, after all, originality.

She snapped the lid back on the pen, then sat down next to

Kitty to watch the news. An aerial view of the Texas university flashed across the screen. Someone's voice, crackling through a broken cell phone line, reported "absolute panic." It was impossible for Hero not to think of Quinn—for a series of unlikely images to run in sequence through her mind. She remembered hearing about this incident briefly, last week, but it had barely registered. She couldn't remember if anyone had ended up dead.

Zoe's face once again splashed onto the screen; she held the camera's gaze steadily. Then, after a slight pause and an audible intake of breath, she announced that a 3.6 magnitude earthquake had shaken the Big Bear region of the San Bernardino Mountains.

Kitty reached over and patted Hero's hand. "That's wonderful, dear," she said. "I'm so glad Quinn's enjoying his school."

Now, Hero wished she had written something—anything—else.

Why, she wondered, hadn't she written something true? "I don't know how to talk to my son." "I walked behind James Turrell's light projection last week and saw the bare bulb, all the tangled-up wires."

She was tired of lying. And pretty well everything she said these days was a lie. How could it not be when she hadn't told anyone—certainly not Kitty—that Quinn was living with Rog now? That her only contact with her son amounted to the roughly two hours they spent together each day in the car, sitting in traffic, in near silence, while Quinn's iPhone played insipid music that actually sounded like it was trying *not* to be heard . . .

But it would have been useless to explain this to Kitty. It would only be a matter of time, a few minutes, maybe, before she would be forced to explain it all over again. Half the time these days, Kitty didn't even remember that Hero and Rog had split up. She'd ask about him as if fifteen years hadn't gone by. Hero had given up trying to correct her. It just didn't do anyone any good, she told herself. Going over it all again, always as if for the first time.

"Yeah. It's a great school," Hero said. "He's liking it a lot."

But these days, even when Hero didn't correct her, she found herself uncomfortably "transported" talking to Kitty. As though it was not just Kitty who occupied an earlier time in her life when nothing that had already happened in it had already happened that way. Questions that she at other times managed to avoid would surface, suddenly, against her will: What had "happened," exactly, Hero would wonder. And when? When had Rog, for example, gone from conceiving of the pool business as a sort of Ed Ruscha meets Robert Smithson experiment in form—"popular land art," he had called it—to a life calling? He didn't make "land art" anymore, no. He made "actual money"— something he had found occasion to remind Hero of more than once even just this past month.

Hero had never made "actual money." But that wasn't what bothered her; she was nearly certain of that. What bothered her was that she hadn't made—or done—anything else either . . . at least not in a long time. When exactly (she would, in Kitty's presence, begin to wonder) had she begun to spend more time making mental lists as to why it was equally valid to cultivate the "aesthetic and creative development" of three-year-olds as it was to cultivate her own? She was still pretty certain her reasoning was correct. The hubris of an artist, especially after a certain age and without any corresponding public reputation, was always embarrassing. But how could one ever really know (she would wonder) if one's own reasoning process wasn't ultimately unreasonable? An irrational desire to make sense of the present despite of, or in accordance with, the past? A way not of perceiving, but instead of forcing the connections, while life itself continued to flash steadily by, in a series of discrete, irreconcilable images . . .

In any case, it was pointless and unfair to want to go back, Hero instructed herself. It just didn't make sense. You couldn't pick and choose like that; you just couldn't.

Hero could smell the asphalt baking even before she got outside. She couldn't wait to get into the car, crank the AC and the radio, get out on the freeway. She'd pick the noisiest radio station she could find, turn up the sound till the car rattled.

But at first she didn't even see her car, and it wasn't that big a parking lot. She considered the idea that the car had been towed, but then she realized it had merely been hidden from view—dwarfed by a large minivan that had pulled into the space beside hers. Stick-figure representations of the family who drove it were plastered to the van's side: Mom, Dad, dog, and three little girls. What purpose, Hero mused, did these representations serve? Was it a way for the family to recognize themselves? Or their vehicle, perhaps? Amid a parking lot potentially full of identical vehicles? Or was it an attempt to communicate something?

And if so, what?

To whom?

She took another few steps. Her own car was, of course, just where she'd left it. Beside it, standing between the driver's door and the van that had concealed the car, was the bride. She was wearing shorts and a T-shirt and was shoving her wedding dress into the van's back seat. As Hero approached, she looked up; flashed a polite grin.

"Sorry."

She gave the van door a tug and it slid shut automatically. Then she turned, in order to make her way around to the driver's side of the van—but Hero was standing squarely in her way.

"Excuse me," the bride said.

Hero didn't budge.

Undaunted, the bride continued to smile. She glanced quickly over her shoulder to see if there was another way out—but there was not. The van's nose had been driven right up to the wall of the Paradise Valley Senior Center and behind her there was just a windowless facade. The bride's expression shifted from embarrassed confusion to vague alarm.

"Excuse me," she said again, and took a step toward Hero. Still, Hero didn't budge. The bride glanced around once more, her eyes, by now, a little wild. Their two figures—facing one another—reflected back at them strangely from the darkly tinted window of the bride's vehicle on one side of them and the darkly tinted window of Hero's on the other.

Once more, the bride took a step toward Hero—this time more assertively—but instead of moving aside, Hero took a step toward the bride so that the two would have collided if the bride had not immediately withdrawn.

"They believe you, you know," Hero said.

The bride shook her head, confused.

"Every week," Hero said. "They *believe you*. They think it's the real thing."

At last the bride seemed to understand what Hero was refer-ring to. It irritated Hero that it took her so long. The bride blinked several times, slowly, then she opened her mouth— seemed about to reply. Before she could do so, however, Hero stepped aside. The bride shut her mouth firmly and hurried past. Hero watched her as she went around to the driver's side of the van, got in, and—without glancing in Hero's direction— backed up the van and drove away.

Hero got into her car, too, and started the engine. She pressed her hands so tightly to the wheel that it wasn't until she'd left the parking lot and merged into the main traffic flow on the freeway that she noticed they were shaking. She'd taken one hand off the wheel in order to fiddle with the air conditioner—though it was already on max and as cool as it could go—and that was when she realized. It was funny. If she'd kept both hands pressed on the wheel the entire drive, exerting just enough pressure on them until the feeling passed, maybe she never would have known they were shaking.

Had she lost her mind? What had she been thinking? Terrorizing a college student! Making a total fool of herself in the Paradise Valley parking lot! What else was she capable of? She imagined swerving into the car next to her, or slamming the brake and bringing the whole line of traffic behind her to a sudden stop. It would take next to nothing; she could almost feel the possibility of it—another moment shuddering beneath or beside the one she was actually inhabiting. What invisible element, she wondered, separated this moment from any other, or from the next . . . ?

She pictured Zoe reporting the story on the six o'clock news: "A single-vehicle accident today involving a forty-seven-year-old white woman disrupted traffic temporarily . . ." With the same calm insistence with which she reported the Dow Jones industrial average. "There is no known cause for the accident. The victim's name has not yet been released."

Hero shook her head to clear it, then put on her blinker to pass a white Jeep ahead of her; New Mexico plates. When she lifted her hand to flick on her blinker she found that her hand was still shaking.

She clicked on the radio, hit the scan button, then looked at the time. It was 2:37; not even rush hour. Maybe there was an accident up ahead. She felt guilty for having imagined causing one only a moment before.

Mostly the scan caught stations during commercial break. Once in a while, a riff of pop country or a top-forty countdown broke through. And now there was the white Jeep—she was somehow behind it again. Talk radio. A Jesus station. More talk radio . . . Didn't anyone, Hero wondered, make noise anymore?

The white Jeep slowed, then stopped entirely. Behind it, Hero hit the brakes and came to a halt just as a commercial for a new auto supply store slid into a strain of stilted gospel. A few people, including the driver of the Jeep—a woman of roughly Hero's own age—got out of their cars. They peered up the freeway, attempting to see what the trouble was up ahead. They conversed together on the side of the road, or else stood by themselves speaking urgently into their cell phones.

Hero should probably call Quinn, tell him she'd be late. Her phone was lying in the console, within easy reach, but she didn't pick it up. She clicked off the car engine instead, disrupting an Emergency Alert test-tone mid-screech. Then she took her hands off the wheel and watched them tremble.

THE
ORIGIN
OF
SPECIES

FOR THE MOST PART, everyone who'd actually seen it agreed that *something* had happened. Just what exactly was more difficult to say. At first, the reporters had come in droves, but then, just as quickly as they came, they went, and after the official report was printed in the *Silver City Tribune*, only the lunatics continued to talk about what had happened that night. Only a few weeks later, nearly everyone seemed to agree that nothing unusual had happened, or was ever likely to happen, in our little town.

But I remember. At one time it was very, very real. And it was headed toward us. Everyone who saw it stopped whatever it was they were doing and piled into their cars, just like Fernie and me. There was a great big line of us, our taillights streaming, heading together out of town. Out past the last gas station and Fulton Wash. It wasn't a decision we made; it was more like an instinct. Like the way that your head turns without even meaning or wanting it to toward a highway accident as you're driving past.

Out past town, the land gets hard and flat and there's no mesquite even. It's just dirt out there, some scrubby creosote, and nothing, not even a rock, for twenty-five miles till the flat-top range. It's true, the mountains look closer than that. It looks like you could just walk out and be at the base of them in something less than an hour. It's funny how the eyes can play tricks on you: that the first known thing on the horizon, whatever it is and no matter the distance, seems close. But at night, there aren't any mountains near or far and darkness is the closest thing. Interrupted only by stars—which, with nothing to compete with out there, are no longer points of light, like in town, but sort of leak out into the rest of the sky—you get this feeling that darkness is just a problem of distance, too. That if you could just see a little farther, it wouldn't be darkness at all.

Fernie and I had been sitting out back of my mother's place. It was just after dark, and Fernie had come by driving Marty's car, a beat-up Impala with the left window blown. We were smoking cigarettes, leaned up against one another, and Fernie was saying something about how nuts it was that you wouldn't know something and then once you did you wondered how you never knew it before.

We were all set to get married that summer—had been engaged by then almost three years, ever since we were sixteen. Living at our parents' places, she at hers, me at mine, and trying to scrape up enough money to leave town. She had learned a new word just that morning, she said, and seen it three times since. She asked me if I knew the word. I don't remember now what it was, but whatever it was I was thinking seriously on it. It was one of those words that you thought at first you knew for sure, but then the more you thought about it the more you realized you didn't know what it meant. I was just realizing this, and Fernie was just in the middle of saying, "I guarantee you, now that I've said it, you'll see this word all over the place, *I guarantee it*"—when we saw the lights.

At first, it was just this hazy glow on the horizon, but then it got brighter and took on more of a definite shape. Fernie said, what the hell, and we both sat up and looked at each other and then back at the sky. Then the light sort of flattened out, and spread itself toward us. It was almost as if—it's weird to say it, even now—it was looking for us. There was a moment when it came so close that we actually ducked. Both of us. And closed our eyes, so we missed it: the actual moment when whatever it was passed right over our heads. I really can't say what would have happened if we hadn't have ducked. If the thing would have hit us or not. If it really was that close, I mean, or that bright, or that real. All I can say is that it felt that way, and that—when we saw it coming—we had no choice but to duck. It was our bodies that made the decision, not our minds. If it had been up to us, we would have continued to stare up at the sky, at that great big ball of light heading toward us, wondering what in the hell it was, what was happening to us. Even if it killed us. We would have just sat there, gaping, with our mouths half-open, like fools. That's the way the mind works, don't ask me why.

Then Fernie said, again, what the hell, and I shook my head and we turned and looked behind us where, in the distance, we could still see the light. It didn't retreat as quickly as it came. It sort of lingered in the sky, and where before it had spread itself out in a single plane, now it seemed to be pressed into the shape of a ball, hovering just above Lucky's Tavern at the far edge of town.

A siren wailed. Then another. Fernie and I looked at each other, then headed back to the house.

My mother was inside. She was sitting at the kitchen table with the newspaper open. Doing a puzzle, I guess, or scanning the swap column for something we didn't need. She didn't appear to have noticed anything.

"We're going out," I said. I tried to make my voice sound light, but it came out high instead. I had this feeling in my throat like something was pressing on it from the inside and if I didn't get moving fast, I was going to explode. But my mother still did not appear to notice anything, and I wonder if, after all, there was nothing unusual in how I sounded. If that was instead the way I always sounded on nights, otherwise just like that one, when Fernie and I got it into our heads to go out together and just drive around.

My mother said only, "All right. Be careful." Without even really looking up, and just in the way that she always said it.

So Fernie and I got into Marty's Impala and headed out toward Lucky's. There were plenty of cars on the road by the time we got out there, and everyone was shouting out the window, "Do you see that? What the hell—?" and beeping their horns at cars that were going too slow because they had their heads hung out the windows, watching the sky. From time to time, a police car or a fire truck screamed past and all the cars pulled off the road and waited for them to go by. It must have taken us the better part of an hour to drive what otherwise would have taken no more than twenty minutes. By the time we got to Lucky's a dozen or so cars were already pulled off the side of the road. The desert is as hard and dry out there as a parking lot, and one after another, cars pulled off the road behind us and everyone piled out and just stood there, or sat on their hoods, and looked up at the great big ball of light, which hovered almost directly above us in the sky. It's sort of funny looking back to remember the lines of police and fire vehicles, and how the cops and the firemen when they got out there had nothing to do but what all the rest of us were doing. Once in a while you could hear the static buzz of a radio, but for a long time there was nothing to report. Fernie and I sat beside one another, perched on the hood of Marty's Impala. From a distance, we saw the Honey twins who were in our same graduating class. Glenn raised his hand in a wave, which Fernie and I returned. For some reason we didn't feel like talking to them, or anyone. Everyone knew everyone else, but people kept to themselves or stood in little groups of two or three, and were mostly silent. We were waiting for something. What, we didn't know—but there was a sort of shared respect for whatever it was, this thing that was happening that we could have in no way anticipated and didn't understand.

Then, slowly—so slowly at first we were not even sure if it was happening—the ball began to descend. Someone pointed and shouted and then there was a sort of murmur of confusion as people tried to decide if anything had happened, or if it was going to, and what they should do if it did. When it became clear that the object had, in fact, moved, and was heading slowly toward us, the policemen grabbed their loudspeakers and told everyone, "Back up, back up!"—but no one moved. The ball, though descending, still seemed far enough away that even our bodies remained riveted, and after a while the cops stopped speaking through the megaphones and we all watched, together, in perfect silence, as the strange ball of light made its first contact with Earth.

I had my heart set on marrying Fernie since the very first day I saw her, at the beginning of seventh grade. She and Marty had just moved from California and Marty had started Desert Trophy, a taxidermy business in the old labour hall off the highway. Sometimes, around town, I say to people who know: "Never dreamed, when I asked her to marry me, I'd get stuck with Marty instead." I say it as if it's a joke. The way Fernie would have said it, I imagine, if the same thing had happened to her. Sometimes that's the only way to treat things. It makes the people around you more comfortable. They think to themselves: good thing he can laugh about it, at least; good thing he's not taking it too hard.

After Fernie was gone—just a few months had passed, six months at most: we were still looking—my number came up. Just like that, it turned up in the first draft lottery of '69. If Fernie had still been around we might have gone to Canada. We'd talked about it, anyway, but just in the way that you talk about a thing that will probably never happen—or at least you figure it won't. It's nice—a strange sort of comfort—to think that things would have been different if Fernie had still been around, but I wonder sometimes if it would have made much difference in the end, or if I would've come, in any case, to the same conclusion: it was just easier to go to the war.

———

We had nothing to do the rest of that summer after Fernie disappeared, Marty and me, except wait around for someone to phone us—Fernie, or somebody to tell us about Fernie. But they never did. I started helping Marty out around the shop, more or less to pass the time, and before long I had learned pretty much everything there was to know about stuffing dead birds and polishing antlers and sewing on glass eyes.

It's good work. And genuinely scientific. A lot of people don't know that. Or this: that if Charles Darwin hadn't been a taxidermist as well as a scientist, the ship he sailed on to the Galapagos—where he made all his famous discoveries—never would have taken him onboard. Who knows? If Darwin hadn't known how to slit open a dead bird then sew it up again, we still might think that we were moulded from clay, or fell out of the sky.

Later, I got a chance to look at the scatter plot of the December draft numbers; the birthdays ran along the vertical axis to the right and the lottery numbers ran horizontal, underneath. All of us, all the guys that got called up, were blue dots, kind of like stars scattered every which way across a blank sky. Some people complained at the time, and afterward. They said the lottery wasn't fair—how they did it, you know. It wasn't random enough. Too many November and December guys got called, they said—because of the way their numbers didn't get mixed in properly, so were still just sitting there, right on top. But when I looked at the scatter plot—all those blue dots floating every which way—it looked pretty random to me. Also, my own birthday is in June, right in the middle of the year. At least from my perspective, you can't really get any fairer than that.

I was the first person in my family to join the service since my great-great-grandfather had fought, and been killed, in the Battle of Antietam, during the Civil War. My father was born with a hole in his heart, which kept him out of the service back in '42. He went to college instead, then came home and worked at the bank and resented every minute of it.

My mother would say, you ought to be grateful, but my father would have gladly turned in every one of his days spent in our small town for a single hour in the service—just enough time to get himself blown up in exactly the way my mother warned him he should be grateful he had not. Sometimes I wondered, if my father had not had a hole in his heart and had instead gone to the war, if he would have been as glad as he thought he would have been, or if, more probably, he would have resented getting killed just as much as he resented not getting killed. Some people are just like that.

Anyway, by the summer of 1967, my father was dead and not from any hole in his heart. He had been killed in a car accident, driving home from work one day—a distance of six miles. My mother hardly spoke or left the house after that, except to go to bingo or to church.

In a way, now that I think about it, it was because of my father—how much he regretted not getting himself killed in the Second World War—that I didn't sign up right away to fight in Vietnam, like nearly everyone else I knew. I didn't want to want anything that my father wanted—but then I didn't want what he didn't want either. So where did that leave me? More than anything else, though, it just didn't seem to make much sense to me, going all the way over to the other side of the world when there were girls like Fernie to marry back home. If my father had still been around, I wonder if he would have given me hell for not joining, and I wonder if that would have made me more likely to join, or less. But my father never mentioned it, even when he still could have. As far as he was concerned, there was only one war, and that was the one in which he should have got himself killed.

By the time I got back, no one talked about the lights and hadn't for a long time. Even the few T-shirts that had been printed, with cartoon alien faces and spaceships, saying, "I survived the UFO landing of 1967," were all in the discount bins, and it was only ever referred to as a sort of a joke.

But Marty and I would still talk about it sometimes. Even though he hadn't been there, he used to ask me to describe what we'd seen. It was always difficult to know exactly what to say. Once I said, "Have you ever seen a beautiful girl walk into the room and you know that your life has been changed?"

He must have known I was talking about Fernie, but at first he pretended not to. He chuckled and said, "Sure. Least a dozen times." So then I said, "Well, then, no, that's not what I mean.

"It's like," I said, "it's like all of a sudden you think that maybe we aren't just put here for the heck of it, though it seems that way most of the time. And it just sort of—surprises you, knowing this all of a sudden, so you can't think straight for a little while."

Marty was looking at me with this funny half smile on his face that after a while turned sad.

"Well, anyway," I said, looking away. "It was like a beautiful girl walking into your life, and you just know that things aren't ever going to be the same."

I heard a lot of guys in Nam talk about death—or near death. Almost everyone had a story to tell, and it was always the same. This bright light in the distance they were either approaching or that was moving toward them.

"No shit," they'd say, "just like they always tell you."

I remember thinking how terrific it was that in the end it all turned out the same for everyone—white guys and black guys, Baptists, Jews. That it didn't matter. You could get shot in the jungle one morning, or slip away, all pumped up with morphine, in the middle of the night, and it would be "just like they tell you." But as comforting as it is to think about death that way, it's also a little unlikely. I don't mean anyone was ever lying, exactly, about what they saw, but just that somewhere along the way all the nuance got lost.

Just as it got lost for all of us back in 1967 when an unidentified object touched the earth. And a light, or a feeling—or something else we hardly had the ability to perceive, let alone understand—shot through us. Even if we didn't believe we'd "made it all up," whatever we'd witnessed that night was so strange—so absolutely unprecedented and unknown—that whenever we spoke of it afterward, we did so by using only the most general terms, and most of us preferred to say nothing at all.

———

The official explanation was that it had been a simple trick of the light. Similar incidents had been reported for centuries, they said. In Texas, there were the "Marfa lights," for example, visible on nearly any calm, cold desert night just outside of that town. The whole thing could be attributed to a sort of optical illusion.

After the report came out, only the lunatics continued to talk about what we had seen as if it had really been "something." If it ever came up in public, we would say, "Oh yeah, wasn't that weird." One of the Honey twins—Neil—ended up with a Medal of Merit during the war, I remember. He had dragged a buddy of his across half a mile of enemy territory, saving his life, and he got interviewed about it afterward, on the national news. When where he was from came up, the interviewer said, "Home of the alien landing, right?" and Neil just laughed. I remember feeling angry about it at the time. So what made you jump into your car that night? I remember thinking. What made you go racing off with your brother to that *exact spot* in the desert, where all of us were waiting, too? What made you stand there with all the rest of us, with your mouth open, looking up at the sky?

There was no note when Fernie left, just a week before we were set to be married. Not then, and not later. No telephone call from the side of a highway somewhere. When we'd run out of places to look and several months had gone by, Marty asked me if I thought, by any chance (he hesitated, an expression on his face like he was apologizing, in advance, for whatever it was he was going to say), there could be a connection between what had happened that night in the desert and Fernie all of a sudden being gone.

Already it was mostly a joke, what had happened, but there were still some pretty wild stories going around. Manny Duncan—who everyone knew had been high on amphetamines at the time—had a particularly intimate one, and that, of course, was the story that got circulated most.

I told Marty no. "What happened that night was just . . . light," I said.

But then I thought about it some more. I couldn't stop thinking about it, and I figured after a while that it had everything to do with Fernie leaving—and Marty knew it even better than me. He'd sensed it somehow, and that was how come he'd continued to ask me about it, even after everyone else had forgotten about it, or explained it away.

To say "light" was just the closest we could come to describing a thing that was bigger than us, that could have been anything, and that we didn't understand. And that was why I knew then that, despite what I told Marty when he asked, it had everything to do with why Fernie was gone. She must have just known something then. I don't know what. She must have seen the way her life had taken, or was just about to take, shape. Known that whatever it was or was going to be was going to be different from the life she had so far known.

And me and Marty, we didn't have any part of it.

So, what about what I knew? How I had felt when Fernie had walked into the room at the beginning of seventh grade and I just "knew" all of a sudden: who I was, and what my life was going to be about, and the fact that nothing would ever be the same? I still wonder about that sometimes, and the closest I can come to making any sort of sense of it is to assume that it's possible that both feelings were—and continue to be—true.

I sit in Marty's studio with the animals all around me, peering at me from the corners and from the high shelves. Some of them are just not finished yet, but others are those that, for various reasons—if they got botched somehow, or the order fell through and we never got paid—we just kept. I know they can't see, but there's something about the look they give me when I glance up sometimes from my work and see them staring back at me that makes me feel like they know something I don't. Even though that's impossible. I took them apart and put them back together again. The eyes they look out at me with, I placed those myself. I extracted their skull and their thigh bones and made replacement parts out of galvanized wire. It's an art, see—a lot of people don't think of it that way. And I pride myself in the fact that, for the best of them, there's no way of telling that the original structure has been cleanly removed from inside.

When I'm not working, I'm waiting for something. Not for Fernie any longer, but for something.

Maybe that's just life, maybe that's just being alive. Or maybe, because of what happened that night—August 12, 1967, which to this day, despite the official report, no one has been able to fully explain—I just keep half expecting something like it to happen again. And really, when you think about it, the odds are pretty good. I mean, what are the chances that something like what happened that night would happen just once and once only, exactly when and where it did, in our little town, where nothing has ever happened? It seems to me more likely that these sorts of things happen all the time and we just don't notice them. Because—I don't know—we're distracted by other things, are momentarily looking away, or don't believe in what we saw.

Other times, though, I prefer to think that what happened really did only happen once. That what we witnessed in the hour we stood out there, watching and wondering what would come next, was the pinnacle of achievement of some distant race, after some unimaginable period of time. That there was no motive, no message, and that the brief moment of contact—in which all of us who had driven out to that exact spot in the middle of the desert stood, mouths gaping, staring up at the sky—was all that it was ever intended to be.

WHAT WE ARE
LOOKING FOR

THE ADVERTISEMENT WAS POSTED ON A THURSDAY MORNING, in the campus publication, The Luminary. "Wanted: Black man, between the ages of 18 and 34."

McKinley had received his MFA and the prestigious Rudy Huff young playwright award just that past spring, for a play praised by the Huff prize committee as a "sharp, funny, and searingly honest" approach to racial profiling in a supposedly "post-racial" world. That same spring, by some miraculous stroke of luck, McKinley had also managed to land an assistant professorship at a small liberal arts college upstate. Six months later, "What We Are Looking For" was scheduled to be performed for the first time by the Woods College inter-session theatre program. Yet another stroke of luck was that McKinley had been granted the funding to bring in the director of his choice to take part in a three-week intensive workshop, leading up to the premiere in the middle of May.

McKinley had, of course, thought immediately of Jules Cassel, his mentor in New York.

When McKinley had first entered the program he'd been dead set on writing a book of short stories—perhaps something he could later turn into a novel—and writing for the theatre had never even crossed his mind. And yet, it was done. It could be, had been, and continued to be done, and Cassel had been the one to look at McKinley squarely over the space of the short table they'd shared off of MacDougal Street one day and tell him so.

"Everyone writes short stories," he'd complained. "Why not try theatre instead?"

Cassel did not say "why not . . ." the way McKinley and everyone else he knew said "why not"—with a sardonic, self-defeating shrug. He said it absolutely sincerely. As though it was not a question at all, but a matter of fact.

It was not therefore the idea itself that inspired McKinley to change his direction, but the way that Cassel presented the option. Sitting there off MacDougal Street, sipping diet ginger ale on ice, and blinking in the sunlight—his expression as blank and unassuming as a child's.

"It's like he's dropped in straight out of the Enlightenment," McKinley told Mary later with an ironic, appreciative smile.

In point of fact, nothing more than a couple of generations separated McKinley and Cassel. They even sort of looked alike. Solid WASPish good looks, unblemished, nondescript but satisfying features, a square if somewhat weak chin. In his second year of graduate school, McKinley had even unconsciously cut his hair in a similar fashion to Cassel's. Though it didn't wave like Cassel's did, though it didn't settle—undeviatingly, and of its own accord—in a perfect seam somewhere just barely left of centre, Mary noticed the similarity right away.

"Oh, hello, Cassel," she'd said when McKinley walked in the front door of the two-room apartment they shared. She said it like Cassel said "why not," straightforward and to the point, but even so, it took McKinley more than a few beats to realize why she'd said it. The words stung more than he liked to admit.

He felt angry, first, and then ashamed—and then, on further reflection, angry again that he should be made to feel either angry or ashamed. There was nothing wrong with Cassel, after all. He'd already had a long and—as they say when someone isn't quite famous—"notable" career. He wrote prolifically; also published, taught, and directed. He'd even produced a few films. A scattering of scholarly articles on the continued relevance of Elizabethan drama had also appeared—articles that McKinley had, several times, cited himself. There was a takedown, for example, of neo-liberal capitalism via Shakespeare's *Timon of Athens*, a critique of President Obama's reluctance to close the Guantanamo detention centre via *Richard III*—all proof that Cassel wasn't entirely out of touch.

And yet there was still something . . . remote about him, McKinley thought. He couldn't quite put his finger on it, but he certainly didn't want to be associated with it, whatever it was. Perhaps mostly because he understood intuitively, without Mary (thank you very much) having to point it out, that Cassel was his best and only option. What more was there, after all, for him than to grow older, more successful; to have his hair, and everything else about him, begin to part itself effortlessly, ever so slightly left of centre . . .

It wasn't inevitable, the way Cassel made it sound. No, in fact, he had only, like, one chance in a billion of actually even making it that far. Things just didn't always work out the way Cassel assumed they "might just as well." Not anymore. Even McKinley's parents, who'd named their only son after the twenty-fifth president of the United States—champion of American industry, promoter of the gold standard, and the last president to serve in the Civil War—had been skeptical, at best, when McKinley told them he was going to major in English rather than the expected pre-med. Certainly, a person had every opportunity to make his own way in the world, his parents had assured him at the time—just so long as he was travelling in the right direction.

In any case, it was a great boon to McKinley that Cassel agreed to be flown upstate in early May, taking time out of his sabbatical year to direct McKinley's play at a college no one had ever heard of.

"I'm sure it will be interesting," Cassel had responded in his one-line email reply to McKinley's somewhat overwrought request.

"What does that mean?" McKinley asked Mary a few seconds after receiving the message. It was first thing in the morning when he opened his email, but when he saw the note he felt like a hundred watts of electricity had just been pumped through him. He'd shot immediately into the kitchen, then hovered impatiently behind Mary as she tended a single fried egg. "Interesting has got to be the least interesting word in the English language," he told her. "I mean, honestly—it should be banned from the vocabulary. It says ab-so-lu-tely nothing."

Mary looked at him, frowned, then went back to her egg—though both of them could see quite clearly that it did not require tending. It irritated McKinley to an unreasonable degree in that moment that someone should spend so much energy on something that did not actually require it.

"But it's good news," Mary said to the egg.

"Well, yes, of *course* it's good news!" McKinley said. He was truly angry now—and hating himself for it. If she had just stopped fiddling with that egg, he thought. Even for a moment . . . If she had just turned, smiled, said, "*Really? Wow!*" in a way like she didn't know everything already, he might have modestly demurred: "Oh, well, we'll see how it goes . . ." Instead, Mary's matter-of-fact response—her demonstrated incapacity to, even for a second, permit her attention to wander from the demands of an egg—had turned him haughty and defensive.

But, really, it wasn't Mary's fault—he knew that. It was Cassel's.

"Honestly," he complained to Mary, "it's like, try punctuation, right? How about a 'Dear McKinley,' a 'Best,' for god's sake. A 'Yours truly.'"

Mary slid a metal spatula under the body of her egg.

"No, really," McKinley said. "*How* is it okay—personally, let alone *professionally*—just to shoot back these one-liners, with no salutation?"

"What are we talking about?" Mary asked.

The egg flipped; the yolk held.

McKinley pouted. "A little common courtesy," he said. "That's all."

Later, over a happy hour red, he said, "What is and is not interesting." They were waiting for two friends from the Art Education Department at the Patio, the coffee shop at the edge of campus that doubled as a wine bar. Everything upstate "doubled" as something else. Nothing was ever just the one thing you wanted it to be.

"That is," he said, "perhaps, and ultimately, the only thing. To be interested. I mean, truly . . ."

"But I do think he means it," Mary offered. She was softer now, kinder than in the morning. After a few more sips of wine, she would soften still more. Their friends would come; she'd begin to laugh. To use her hands when she spoke, to flash her eyes this way and that. He'd begun to notice it. That she only really turned on when other people were around now. It had dawned on him slowly, but now he couldn't help but be certain of it, and he didn't know if it should bother him. Perhaps it was just one of those things, inevitable after seven years with any one person.

What did he expect? *Seven years!* It was a number that suggested having come to a certain decision—about, for example, with whom one was going to spend the next seven years. He guessed that he and Mary had as good as decided, but they'd never even come close to saying so out loud. Decisions had always been made step by step between them, circumstance to unforeseen circumstance. Up until this point things had just "made sense." It had made sense, for example, for them to begin to share an apartment four years ago because New York was so goddamn expensive and they both hated their roommates. More recently, it had made sense for Mary to accompany McKinley upstate because she was sick of the city and worked freelance so could really be anywhere she pleased.

He'd always anticipated—perhaps even vaguely hoped— that there would come a point when they would actually have to "decide." More lately, though, he'd begun to suspect that before he ever really "made a decision" about anything in his life he would already have quietly begun to live out the consequences of the ones he had already made. As now, for example, when he suddenly realized that, even though he and Mary had never once talked about marriage except in the most oblique ways—referring to the things that "other people" did—chances were they would end up sticking it out with one another, and in more or less the same way that "other people" did.

It was not Mary herself, or the idea of being with her for the next seven or fourteen or however many years into the future, that worried him. It was the fact that his future began to look . . . probable. Yes, he could suddenly see himself quite clearly at this exact same table thirty years from now, waiting for the same couple to arrive, with Mary beside him like a lamp—to be turned on only when the company arrived.

Gail and Jeff. Museum studies folk, both of them. Gail had just got tenure and Jeff was up this year; he'd sort of submerged lately, gone underground in that academic way. In this business, when someone disappears, it's perfectly normal, even condoned. And when they resurface a couple of months later, thinner, or heavier, depending on their constitution, something unhealthy about the eyes, no questions are asked.

"You're being cynical." (Mary.)

As a writer, McKinley considered it his duty to keep a certain grasp on what he called real life—a category that included food, drink, sex, and *actual* conversation. (When Mary pressed him on his definition of the latter, he replied that it was indefinable—that you specifically should not be able, at the end of an "actual" conversation, to itemize topics discussed.) "Real life" also included a few vigorous hikes in the mountains (because despite various trends in how to approach or convey it, one thing that never went out of fashion was a good dose of the SUBLIME) and, for good measure, a bus ride now and then, even when one owned, for the first time in one's life, a perfectly good vehicle, on which one made sizeable monthly payments.

The date they were keeping tonight was one that had been postponed by a month and a half. Jeff had said: "February is really busy."

"February?" McKinley had exclaimed to Mary. "How can a whole month be busy?"

And yet suddenly his own life was beginning to pass by like this, in swaths.

Gail and Jeff arrived apologizing, bringing the cold air in from the street. They undressed, piling their sweaters and scarves over the backs of their chairs. Gail looking a little thinner, or maybe it was just the light. Jeff, perhaps a little heavier.

"So, so, so . . . How's everything with you?" (Jeff.) Like he was running his finger down a page, looking for a place to begin.

"Not so very good" would have been McKinley's honest response. He was often in the habit of taking people at their word when they asked, "How's things?"

Mary had instructed him on this. "You know no one actually wants to know how you are, don't you?" she'd asked him once. "It's just like saying 'Hello' when you pick up the phone. You're supposed to reply, simply, 'good,' 'fine,' 'all systems go.'"

"But why?" McKinley had asked. "Why bother going to all the trouble of establishing a connection if you're not ever allowed to actually say anything?"

Of course, he *got* it. He knew what Mary meant. He'd been practically named after the gold standard, for god's sake. And he always felt it acutely afterward—after he'd broken what Mary called the "social contract," and everyone had awkwardly bundled back into their coats and headed back into the cold. He would be left to finish off his drink and shrug back at Mary across the table—his forehead wrinkled as though he was trying to remember something, and wondering what happened.

"We're looking for a black man between the ages of eighteen and thirty-four," McKinley told Jeff. "We can't find one. We can't find a single young black man in the tri-county area willing to perform the role."

They'd put out the initial advertisement in *The Luminary*, then the local newspaper, the TV station, the radio. McKinley had printed out the casting call and posted it at the gym, the library, the pizza place, the coffee shop. He gestured to the community bulletin board behind them where the call was barely observable beneath handwritten advertisements for roommates, lost cats, and hot yoga. "Wanted," the ad read: "Black man, between the ages of 18 and 34, *for leading male role in a new play by the award-winning playwright McKinley Scott.*"

No one had called. He'd talked to his colleagues—implored them to put him in touch with any young black men they knew who might have an unexplored interest in the theatre. "No experience necessary!"

They'd looked at him quizzically. *You actually want me to approach a young black man,* their looks seemed to suggest, *say, "You're just the type . . ."?*

When McKinley stared back at them, in a way that suggested, *Yes. That's exactly what I want you to do,* they'd smiled and nodded, avoided looking him in the eye.

It certainly was a shame that there wasn't a bigger pool for McKinley to draw from in such a small town, they said. It must be a shock, coming from the city. But wasn't that showbiz. You never could guess the sort of problems you'd run into along the way . . .

"So, what are you going to do?" (Gail.)

McKinley shrugged. "I've given myself till the end of the week," he said. "Then I have to decide if I'm going to cancel or not. Just—cancel the whole thing."

"But isn't . . ." Jeff cleared his throat. He looked embarrassed. "I mean, if I'm understanding you right, isn't this precisely what you're trying to get away from?" He shifted in his seat, looked anxiously for some reason at Gail across the table. "I mean," he began again, "if the play is a critique of the way that, you know, we're all expected, or required, to play a set role based on our . . . social and cultural backgrounds, then maybe this is an opportunity for the play to actually function as a critique. I mean, maybe it would be interesting to open the role up a little—" Again, he looked nervously at Gail, then at McKinley.

Everywhere but Mary.

Mary took a sip of her wine. "Yes," she said, "why don't you give the white folks a chance, McKinley?"

But she said it in a way that everyone knew she was joking.

Jeff even laughed, a little—apologetically. Grateful for having been, at once, both assigned the blame and relieved of it.

"We've thought about it," McKinley said quickly. "Believe me, we've thought of *everything*." He heaved a sigh and, then, with exaggerated nonchalance: "Even of taking things back to the minstrel days."

Dead silence.

"Blackface," McKinley explained.

Gail gave a startled laugh, and shot a glance at Mary. Mary was rolling her eyes—indicating both her consent and dismay. Purposely (McKinley thought), she did not look at him. No doubt she was thinking, like he was, of his latest idea, which he had sprung on her the previous night.

He had been waiting for her when she came in from shopping that evening; had practically leapt at her before she was even properly in the door. "You'll play the part!" he said, extending his arms like a game show host presenting first prize.

Mary looked at him blankly. She was still clutching a bag of groceries in each hand. In his excitement he hadn't thought to relieve her of them.

"Yes!" McKinley had said, still fuelled by his own energy, though he must have known immediately that something was wrong. The barometric pressure of the room had dropped sharply, but Mary just looked at him—her grip tightening on the grocery bags she had not yet set down. It was almost as if she was willing him to take it back—willing him to establish for both of them that what he'd said had been intended only as a bit of a joke, just like almost every other idea they'd come up with so far.

But McKinley was absolutely serious. The idea had struck him—and in that moment it still did—as a beautiful solution. It was not until Mary, in a small, hard voice McKinley had never heard before, said, "I'm not an actor, McKinley," set down the groceries, and left the room, that he fully realized his mistake.

But still he hadn't acknowledged it. They'd eaten dinner in silence. Immediately after the plates had been cleared, Mary had brought out her laptop and begun to type furiously. She was always working toward one deadline or another. Still, though, she went to bed earlier than McKinley, and when he got into bed she was turned away from him, on her side. He'd touched her waist briefly, and she'd groaned a little—indicating that she was, or should be considered to be, asleep.

"I love you, Mary," he said. Quietly, almost under his breath. Not "I'm sorry." What good did those words ever do? That was another of their running debates. Mary thought it at least established a point from which to begin "a new conversation"; he thought it was nothing more than a way of sweeping things under the rug.

Now, though, in the wine bar, he found himself hoping—a little desperately—that his exaggerated emphasis when he'd said "We've thought of *everything*" would serve as an apology of sorts.

Perhaps he would even do so officially. He felt suddenly inspired—eager to "start a new conversation," even to sweep things under the rug, if that's what it took!

He'd apologize later, he promised himself. After Gail and Jeff went home and he and Mary were left to shrug ruefully over their glasses of wine and walk home together in the cold.

"What about if you . . . make it part of the story?" (Gail.) "I mean, what if you were self-conscious about it? You could even make a note in the program about how hard you looked. It might open people's eyes, in the way, you know—like it sounds like the play is trying to do . . ."

She trailed off; of course, she hadn't actually read the play. Almost nobody had. Everyone knew about it, had heard something about it, had been "meaning to," but very few people had actually read it. This meant that it was always discussed in very general terms. McKinley had even begun to think of it this way. Less as a play and more as an idea of a play.

Perhaps that was part of the problem. A *specific* play could be performed, but not a "play" in general.

"Yeah," Jeff said, "and you could write yourself in somehow, too. And—all of this. First, your writing of the play, what you *intended*, then the difficulty of transferring that intention to the stage . . ."

"Words into action," Gail said.

"Because, of course," Jeff said, "the whole point is to get us to look at the construct rather than the individual. To show us how the construct gets made."

"Mmm," McKinley said. But he felt suddenly confused. Even without having read his play, what Jeff was saying about it was true—and yet somehow the way it sounded coming out of Jeff's mouth was all wrong.

Besides, the whole "point" of actually staging the production, rather than simply writing the play, was for the role he'd constructed to become *an actual person* rather than a mere description, an empty casting call fluttering about on a community bulletin board in the breeze.

"And yet even the individual is a construct," Jeff said, "and that, it seems to me, could be used to your advantage—if you chose to look at it that way. I mean, even if you do manage to find someone to fit the description, so to speak, you might avoid"—here he faltered—"certain difficulties, which naturally arise whenever anyone attempts to speak from someone else's perspective or experience . . . If you wrote yourself into the play, it would be a way of—how would you say it—?"

"Bracketing," suggested Gail.

Mary nodded. She was not looking at anyone in particular— was just nodding in the way that she always did when she wanted to suggest attention. McKinley knew this instinctively, but in actuality he had never been able to catch Mary out not listening to something when she appeared to be.

"Yes, sure," Jeff said, "bracketing—or, or framing—your own perspective so that we can see that it's not a question of positing one particular point of view or, or presuming to speak—"

"But, lest we forget," McKinley said, holding up his hand like a preacher or a traffic cop. "I am presuming to speak."

They looked at him. It is remarkable how many places there are to look even in a small room, seated around a smallish table, in the company of only three others. How many angles there are, near or approximate, to actual direct eye contact with another human being; how variously attention and contact can be feigned without its ever being accurate exactly to say so. Because it was only by sudden contrast with the moment in which, after McKinley said "Lest we forget" in that exaggerated and preposterous way and drew them all up short so that they *actually looked at him*, that it was possible to observe that they hadn't actually been looking at him before.

"That's the entire point of theatre, isn't it?" McKinley said. "I mean why I wrote the play at all. I am, God help me, actually trying to speak *for someone else*. I am quite literally putting words in *somebody else's* mouth."

All three of his companions stared at him. They looked torn between sympathy and condescension. He could sense the well-meant but dismissive discussion that would take place afterward as Gail and Jeff walked home.

"A bit *naive*," Jeff would say. "And something of a loose cannon."

"Honestly," Gail would add, "I wonder how Mary puts up with it."

Maybe Mary herself was wondering that now. It didn't fail to occur to McKinley, despite or because of how comfortable their relationship had lately become. If Mary should leave him . . . But he couldn't finish the thought. His mouth tasted suddenly sour, and his stomach went cold. He felt, in advance, the terrible blow it would be. How the "opportunities" he had sometimes offhandedly considered of being single again (watching shitty TV at the end of the day instead of the news, travelling more, sleeping with men, going to shows) would seem suddenly terribly stark. More than with any other human being, he had been given a chance with Mary. There had been times when he had actually felt it in his body: how close they had come to actually "getting through." But almost inevitably when he felt this way he would find a way to ruin it somehow. As if he physically required the reintroduction of the distance that had diminished between them. He would get his back up about something, purposely misunderstand her, turn away, become chilly and need a sweater, anything to become himself again, to re-establish the borders.

Of all of them, Gail was the least torn. She was looking at him now with outright condescension, as though he'd just outed himself as a climate change denier. Gail, whose latest work was a reflection on the emotional life of rocks. A recent show, "Making the Stone Stony Again," had received national attention and was at this moment no doubt being discussed across the country by graduate students interested in speculative philosophy, systems thinking, and super-realism. Gail, who was seriously contemplating the emotional life of a rock, was looking at him as though he had a screw loose because he deigned to speak for another human being.

"Of course," Gail said.

Jeff took a piece of sourdough bread from the basket that had recently been delivered to their table and tore off a piece with his teeth. Mary burst out laughing.

"What's so funny?" McKinley said. He felt like a kid who'd been left out of a joke. It was not an unfamiliar feeling. He'd always been the one to force an explanation, instead of just letting it go. Even though he was aware of how irritating this was; how, of course, the joke wasn't funny once it had to be explained. But he was simply incapable of letting the joke just happen without him, and suspicious that other people only faked good humour most of the time, because he didn't understand how he was the only one in the world who didn't get jokes.

"I'm going to call off the play." (McKinley.)

Mary stopped laughing. "What?" She was still holding on to the tablecloth and looked genuinely confused.

"Oh, but McKinley," Gail said—suddenly more sympathy than snobbery—"that would be . . . sad."

"It does seem that there ought to be a solution," said Jeff.

"Yes," Mary said. "Though, at the same time." She paused, looked at him. "McKinley's put so much into this play. He cares about it deeply. It's hard to know whether it would be better to perform it in less than ideal circumstances and risk it not exactly coming across, or not to perform it at all."

"Or not yet, anyway," Gail offered.

"That's true," said Mary. Again she looked at McKinley. Kindly, McKinley thought. Apologetically, perhaps. Aware that she had hurt him with her laughter, which he had failed to understand.

"It's a real dilemma," Jeff said, in a voice that indicated he was ready, as all of them were ready by now, to discuss something else. "I'm curious what you will do, McKinley. It seems clear that in this situation, as in so many, there really is no right answer."

"But that doesn't mean," Mary said, "that there isn't a wrong answer. It's this, after all, that McKinley's play does such a beautiful job of pointing out."

Was it? McKinley realized that he had absolutely no idea what his play was about.

"The play doesn't just throw up its hands like everything else," Mary was saying. "It's interested in why things happen, and continue to happen, the way that they do—why we're stuck in this pattern, this loop. It doesn't just take a step back, though—point to the loop, and say, 'Isn't that interesting.' It wants to find a way out."

McKinley could almost have cried he was so grateful to Mary
at that moment. But he felt confused, too—unsettled. Like
maybe Mary was talking about somebody else's play. After all,
he thought, bewildered and a little ashamed, if his play was, like
Mary suggested, about why things happened the way they did,
shouldn't he—its author—have to this question at least some
provisional reply?

And as for a way out . . . He thought desperately, but for
the life of him he couldn't recall dropping a single clue as to the
direction one might move in. Was he, he wondered, a small panic
rising in him at the thought—deep down—truly *interested* in the
subject of his play, or had he found it merely "interesting"? Had he
really considered, the way Mary had said that he had, the question
of *why*—or had he, like Cassel, merely deferred the question?

"It's a real dilemma," Jeff said again. Again his tone, which
included a barely detectable sigh, indicated that he was ready to
talk about other things.

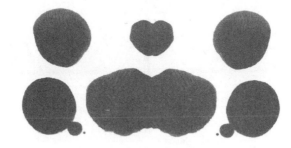

WEATHERMAN

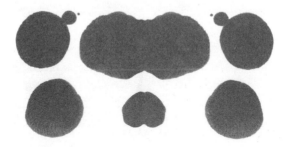

"IT'S THE SAME EVERY MORNING. The alarm beeps, I slam it shut, then I slide out of bed. I have to be careful to get up quickly. If I wait too long, my brain starts to kick in; I start thinking about how ungodly it is to wake up at this hour, and then about what would happen if, just this once, I simply turned over and went back to sleep.

"I start to picture everyone flapping around at the studio, wondering what to do, slamming drawers and shuffling pages and snapping at one another. I picture Stacy, the intern, being shoved on the set at the very last minute and stumbling her way through the morning report. I picture the phones ringing off the hook afterward, everyone wondering if the daytime high is eighty-two degrees in Tucson and eighty-eight in Benson, or the other way around.

"I could call in sick, of course—that would prove only slightly less dramatic. I have not used a single sick day this year, and in fact have only ever used five sick days in my entire career. Some people find this pretty unbelievable, but it's true. Five sick days and on a single occasion, back in the early nineties, when my appendix burst on set. I know exactly the moment it happened. I'd had this searing pain in my gut all morning, and then—I was staring into the camera, still smiling, waiting for the cut—the pain just sort of gave way. It was like a wave rolling back. I could feel my smile flex at the edges; I had to hold on to the rim of the desk in order not to float away. Finally, I got the all-clear sign, and got up and drove myself to the hospital. I was out for a week.

"If I get up right away, as soon as—or even just a half beat before—the alarm goes off, it's all pretty automatic. I snap off the alarm and slide out of bed—careful not to disturb Regina. My slippers are next to the bed and my robe is on the chair, next to the slippers. I slide into these (robe first, then slippers) and head to the guest bedroom across the hall. I use the guest bathroom to shower, shave, and brush my teeth, and the bedroom to dress. All my clothes have to be laid out the day before—everything pressed and ready, lined up neatly on the bed. If I'm not careful, and something goes wrong—like I find a stain on my shirt, or I've forgotten my socks and have to start rooting around for them in the drawer—I can get a little suicidal. I imagine suffocating myself, for example, amongst two hundred identical button-down shirts, or strangling myself with a striped tie. What a shock it would be, I think, for Regina to find me that way when she finally wakes up—sometime after eight o'clock. In all probability, though, Regina wouldn't be the one to find me. She has no cause to use the guest room as she disturbs no one, getting dressed at such a reasonable hour. She'd probably just go about getting ready for her day as usual. Blow-dry her hair, fix a light breakfast, some coffee; wonder briefly why I'd decided to forgo mine. You'd think finding the car in the drive would alert her that something was up, but no—. Regina is so infinitely reasonable that she would probably just assume I'd decided to get a lift into the studio with Mark, who is also on the morning show, and lives nearby. Have I ever once done this? No. Mark's mentioned it a couple of times, but Regina knows how I feel about the idea. Still, with the car in the drive, it's the only reasonable explanation. I must—Regina will think—have gotten a lift with Mark, who (just as I might have anticipated) disrupted my morning routine to such an extent that I was able neither to drink my coffee, nor turn off the warmer under the cup.

"Realizing this, Regina will flick off the warmer and go off to work herself. So it will be Amira, the cleaning lady, and not Regina, who will find me—either suffocated or hanged in my closet—when she comes in at noon.

"Regina will receive the call at work . . . She'll listen, lips parted, eyes darting—bewildered—around the room. Then she'll put the phone down. She is so eminently reasonable that at first she won't believe it. Afterward, she'll tell her friends: I didn't believe it. Her voice will be breathless, soft; her eyes filled with tears that never actually spill . . .

"This is why I'm careful to put my clothes out the night before. If everything is laid out ahead of time, I can be dressed in under two minutes and I don't have time to think about anything save whatever is absolutely necessary to allow me to get fully dressed in under two minutes. I can go to the kitchen, where my cup of coffee—set on the automatic setting for 5:00 a.m.—is already brewed. I can click off the warmer, grab the cup of coffee, and—without thinking—walk out the door."

———

I tell all of this to Dr. Yaun. She sits across from me, behind a large desk, kept pretentiously bare, nodding and frowning just slightly, so as to suggest attention rather than disapproval. From time to time she shifts in her chair, leans an elbow on the edge of the empty desk, and places a single finger just above her chin. She's attractive; about my own age, I would guess—nearing forty. Though it is difficult to tell with women. She isn't Asian, as her name would suggest. She must have married an Asian man and figured that the outdated trend of professional women taking their husband's name was balanced by the progressive trend of interracial marriage.

She has been recommended by Greer, who for all intents and purposes is my boss—though she doesn't like to call herself that. She's the senior producer of the morning show, but likes to foster what she calls a sense of "workplace equality." No one, she says, is worth any more or less. We're a team where everyone (a brief pause here for a moment of deliberate eye contact all around) is Most Valuable Player. It is no coincidence that the equality bullshit started just after September 11, when my own ratings went through the roof.

It wasn't just me. For some reason—who can say why exactly—sometime right after September 11, people all across America just started loving weathermen. It happened slowly at first, then—*bam*—I woke up one morning and I was a celebrity. I got fan mail from all over the state, then from all over the nation. I couldn't keep up. I typed up a stock response on program stationery, which the intern signed, folded, and mailed away:

I'd like to personally thank you for
your support and appreciation of our
show. It fills me with a deep sense of
pride and satisfaction to be able to
deliver reliable weather reports to
you every morning.

There was even a point—sometime in the mid-2000s—when I was being stalked by this group of young women. I'm not kidding. They would hang out behind the station's back door most mornings, waiting for me to emerge. They brought T-shirts, notebooks, even—yes, at least once—a lacy undergarment for me to sign. Which I did, with an appropriately modest smile.

Greer was over the moon at first; my popularity did wonders for the network's ratings. But then I noticed a shift in her attitude. It was as though it was suddenly my fault I was getting all this attention—even though she was behind the whole thing, pushing it as far as it would go. We had plastic dolls made, and snow globes with gold flakes of sand instead of snow and a half-inch figure approximating me standing next to a saguaro cactus. When you shake it, the gold dust swirls then falls, like thermonuclear fallout, finally coming to rest on our outstretched limbs.

"You asked me before why I thought there was all this fuss suddenly about weathermen. I guess I always just figured it was because everything else in the world is so uncertain. That the weather is going to change is the one thing we can, with any

confidence, rely upon. Also, it's not personal. The weather has
nothing to do with you. You can't change it, or even really pre-
pare for it, aside from in the most limited ways. You just have
to wait and see. Check in with the weatherman, see what he
knows. Half the time he's wrong, of course, but then, that's all
right, too. Sure, people complain—I get it all the time. But it's
also a sort of a joke. No one ever really blames a weatherman.
No one holds it against him if he tells you, 'chance of rain,' and
then it doesn't rain—especially in the desert.

"I used to think that was the problem. My ratings were just
as good or better than a lot of the guys working in the Northeast
or the tornado belt, or along the Gulf, but I couldn't help but
think there would be more overall—how should I put it?—job
satisfaction—a sense of purpose, I suppose—in a location
where I had more to report. I would watch the guys out in
Kansas, for example, reporting floods and hurricanes; study the
way they conveyed the news. With the good ones, there was
never even a ripple of alarm. They had the resignation of news-
casters—but they had something else, too. Because the thing
about the weather is, it's not like the news; it's not about reporting what already happened somewhere. It's prophetic; it's an art.
Watching those guys, I was even more sure of it. Like, remember a while back, Oklahoma getting slammed with—I don't
know—something like three or four tornadoes right in a row? It
was like the Last Judgment. It must have felt like that out there,
anyway. They must have just been waiting for it—for the sky to
turn black, and start charging. You'd turn on your television
because you'd be looking for someone to warn you—to explain
to you when it was coming, and why.

"Because the weather isn't about resignation, like the evening news. There's a practical urgency to it; simple steps to be taken. If a weatherman is good, all the wisdom of the ages can be conveyed through an appropriate gesture, a well-chosen phrase. Even his physical presence (framed by complex, uninterpretable weather patterns swirling beyond) should suggest strength and resolve. Fairness, too. If a weatherman is good, he should be able to convey a sense of there being certain parameters, not only to expectation and desire, but also to ignorance and loss."

There is such a very long pause that after a while I give up on the idea that Dr. Yaun will actually respond. But then she does. "And so, what you're saying," she says, finally, "is that it's the *stability* of the weather conditions here that you began to . . . resent."

"Yes, exactly," I say. "I began to resent living in a place where, even in the winter, the temperature hardly dips below fifty degrees. I began to feel that it was . . . deeply meaningless to live in a place where the weather is predictable, where on almost any given day I can be counted on to report, 'sunny, clear skies.' I watched those guys out in Kansas and Oklahoma, in New York after Sandy, in Ohio after yet another bad flood, and I started to—"

I shift position, sinking even lower into the deep cushions of Dr. Yaun's armchair. I've gained quite a lot of weight recently, and my extra pounds help to pin me among the chair's soft folds. I realize it will now take a noticeable effort to extract myself.

Dr. Yaun nods encouragingly, but I've lost my train of thought; I can't finish my own sentence.

Dr. Yaun doesn't say anything either. She just sits there, looking at me, pinned to my chair, and for almost three full minutes (which I watch tick by slowly at the end of one of my outstretched arms) we sit together in near-perfect silence.

I think about how rare that is. How we're always so eager to complete our own, or each other's thoughts—to fill in the gaps, finish sentences. It was a particular habit of mine, in fact—finishing other people's sentences. When you work in television long enough, you start to hear every extra beat. Even off camera it gets so you can't stand it, listening to people hem and haw as they hunt for the right expression, or word. Whenever I can I always jump in and supply one. My last intern, Jeff, for example—I don't know how many hours I would have lost out of the three full months he worked at the studio if I had waited patiently, like Dr. Yaun, for whatever it was he was trying to say.

This habit irritated Regina—I knew that. "Just—listen, for chrissakes, will you?" It was one of the many things in our relationship I was supposed to be "working on." There were so many of them—things I needed to "work on" and things we needed to "work on together"—I had trouble keeping track. But she didn't. She always noticed. Women do. In general: they notice things. It would continually amaze me, for example, going over to other people's houses with Regina, or watching something on television. How afterward she'd want to discuss all these little details about other people's lives: their personal idiosyncrasies, their subtle flaws—all things I hadn't noticed, and never would have, if she hadn't mentioned them. Once she did, I'd have to admit she was right, though. She almost always was.

And yet—strangely, she hadn't noticed anything about my own behaviour over the past few months, which even I knew had been a little odd.

Even Mark, who was hardly what you might call perceptive, was always giving me the look: a raised eyebrow and half a smile. On anyone else it would've seemed like he'd just told a bad joke and was waiting for the delayed reaction—a groan, or an ersatz guffaw—but it was probably the closest Mark ever came to expressing genuine concern.

It wasn't anything really bad. It was just—I'd started acting different. I'd drift off—stare into space sometimes, for no reason. Laugh too long or too hard at something that wasn't funny. Notice only after everyone else—embarrassed—had turned with renewed purpose back to their work.

I knew it was odd. "Out of character." But honestly, I didn't think too much about it, except to feel vaguely annoyed whenever Mark gave me one of his looks. Then, out of the blue, Greer called me into her office and slipped me Dr. Yaun's card. "She's simply the best," she said as she slid the card across her desk. "I just know she could help you to manage your . . . stress."

I remember I just stared. I was genuinely surprised. So I drifted off sometimes, I remember thinking. So what?

"I'm fine," I said. And laughed. Not long or hard or anything. Just a quick, totally standard, guffaw. I kept waiting for Greer to shrug and laugh, too; to say something like, "Oh great, Tom, I just, you know, have to offer the option to every employee . . . that sort of thing!"

But she didn't.

"I've never really been into that sort of thing," I joked. "Plus, I'm fine. Really." I was still staring at her—trying to figure her out. Regina would have known what was up in a flash. One look at Greer looking at me and she would have said something like, "She's acting like *such and such*, but underneath she's feeling *such and such*, and because of that, you can tell what she's really after is *such and such* . . ." But I just saw—Greer. Looking at me like she always did. Maybe a touch more tired—a little "stressed" herself. Makeup a bit shiny in places.

"Greer . . ." I said. Then—I can't explain it. Maybe it was something about the way she was sitting, sort of leaned in, so that I could see the way her pores showed beneath her makeup; how they refused to be concealed. I felt tender toward her all of a sudden, almost unbearably close. It was impossible, I thought, that she wouldn't understand . . .

"Greer . . ." I said again. And in another moment I would have told her everything. About how some days I didn't even hear the alarm go off. I would get up automatically and realize only after I was already standing that I'd missed it by a single beat. About how I had to be careful to buy new pants before the old ones didn't exactly fit me anymore because there is nothing—I was this close to telling Greer—like trying to button a button at the top of pants that are just a little too tight to induce in me a now familiar desire to strangle myself with one of my striped ties.

"Greer . . ." I said again.

But in ordinary life, you can't hesitate like that. You can't start a single sentence three times. Someone is bound to cut you off.

"Look, Tom," Greer said. "If you don't call Dr. Yaun and get some help immediately, we're going to have to start looking at other options."

It was the way she said "other options" that brought me back to earth. I got angry then. For a few moments I could hardly see straight I was so mad. Of course, I thought. It's the extra weight. I'd practically made her career for her and here was Greer ready to have me committed because I'd put on a few extra pounds. "If it's—" I began, but I was ashamed to even say the words out loud. I tried again. A different approach this time. "My ratings haven't gone down," I said. "They haven't gone up in a while, but they're steady."

"Tom," Greer said. She pointed to the card with Dr. Yaun's name and telephone number on it, then nodded toward the door.

It's funny: you'd think—especially back in the early 2000s, with the weatherman craze—I would've had lots of opportunities to get myself into compromising situations with women, but the only genuinely compromising situation I'd ever gotten myself into was with Greer.

It was a few years ago now. She'd called me into her office one day; said, just like this time, that she wanted "a word." But it wasn't a word that she wanted, and I had a hell of a time extricating myself. I don't think I've ever had a more compli- cated feeling. Sleeping with Greer had never occurred to me before that moment, except in the most banal of ways—but suddenly I had never desired anything more. And yet . . . I was afraid. I almost panicked, to tell you the truth. I kept seeing myself from above, thinking, *This is how it happens; how you sleep with your boss* . . . But I wasn't really in the frame. I kept sort of shifting out of it, and nothing was in focus, and after a while everything felt—just totally off. I wanted to sleep with Greer more than anything, but I wanted to do it . . . some other time. I wanted to "be prepared." I told her that; used those words, even. I didn't want to hurt her feelings.

In the movies, people are always calling each other into their offices for "a word" that is suddenly—without any words—not "a word" at all, but in real life everything happens more slowly. You can't cut, like in the movies, from one frame to the next, leaving out all the clumsy details. Even if you're lucky and you manage to be suave and well behaved the whole time, there's still all those slow seconds ticking by, the accompanying inner mono-logue that, thankfully, most movies have the prudence to cut. In real life, even desire is not even really desire, pure and simple, the way it is on the screen. It's this mixed-up thing instead, which—if my experience with Greer is any indication—doesn't even have to do with a particular person, or the situation at hand. It's more just this . . . curiosity, about what's going to happen next. A sort of sick, vertigo-provoking longing to induce the unexpected.

Maybe other people had an easier time of it. Greer, for exam-ple. She has this certain script that she follows, I bet, and can count on people, for the most part, to just sort of follow along.

But then I'd gone and asked for a rain check. Ha. You can bet I didn't get it. Greer hardly spoke to me for six months after that, I remember, and made sure I felt like squirming whenever she was in the room. It's hard not to start to slowly despise

someone who makes you feel that way. I'm sure the feeling was
mutual, but until Greer handed me Dr. Yaun's card across the
table I had never once thought about the possibility of losing
my job.

I stood outside Greer's office with Dr. Yaun's card in my
hand and it was clear as day to me, suddenly, how things would
transpire. I wasn't being sent to Dr. Yaun for "rehabilitation";
I was being let go. Greer had, no doubt, been waiting for the
opportunity ever since I'd backed awkwardly out of her office
three years ago after the world's most humiliating handshake.
She'd been biding her time, just waiting for me to show the least
sign of weakness.

"Well, this has been a very worthwhile session," Dr. Yaun informs
me. Her voice surprises me. I'd been, more or less covertly, looking at my watch the whole time, but somehow hadn't registered
just how close we now are to the end of the session.

"I'll see you next week, then?" Dr. Yaun asks. "Same time?
Does that work for you?"

It's a lot easier than I thought it would be to get up from the
chair. Dr. Yaun gets up, too. She moves around the broad desk
and offers me her hand. I take it and find that it is strangely
cool. "I want you to remember, Tom," she says, still shaking
my hand, "you're not alone. It may feel like you are," she says,
"but you're not."

Then she releases my hand, and flexes her own hand a little—
an insignificant gesture that somehow seems to cancel out the
small moment of professional intimacy we've shared. It is really

just the slightest of movements, hardly discernible. But I notice. I have a sudden insight into what it would be like to go around the world like Regina, noticing everything. I can almost see the thoughts as they tick through the doctor's mind: *Some sympathy, now. Careful to keep it professional. Running a bit late; doesn't matter. Make him feel—safe. First visit, and all that.* Maybe that's selling her a bit short. After all, she does seem—aside from that subtle, no-doubt-mostly-unconscious flex of the hand—genuinely sympathetic.

That's the trouble with noticing everything. You never know if the things you notice are real or if they're just things you make up in your head.

It's better then, in a way, not to notice, I think. That way you don't have to always be wondering.

"Do you have any hobbies?" Dr. Yaun asks. I look at her sort of blankly, and don't immediately respond. This time, though, she doesn't wait. Our time is up, after all. "You know, I always prescribe exercise," she tells me. "Really. The research is pretty conclusive. In most cases, a little exercise does just as much good as an order of prescription medication."

Somehow I am out the door. I'm standing in the lobby again. There's an older woman in the chair I'd been sitting in an hour before, while I waited for my name to be called. She's wearing sunglasses, carrying a red umbrella, and flipping through a magazine. The receptionist lifts her head. "We've got you scheduled for next week," she assures me. "Have a nice day."

Exercise. I wonder briefly if Greer told her to say that. But then I think: that's ridiculous. "Do a little exercise and call me in the morning." Like the doctor said, the evidence is in: pretty much anyone would prescribe it these days. And anyway, Greer isn't looking to "help" me, is she? This isn't a makeover. It's a way of showing me the door.

How, I wonder, will I break it to Regina?

I think this as I'm heading down the short staircase to the glass lobby of the building and suddenly the stairs start to seem incredibly steep and narrow. It sounds crazy, I know it, but I can hardly see my way to the bottom anymore. I stand there, with my hand on the rail, breathing heavily—like an old man. There's no way forward, I think. But then I think, no. That's wrong. I've got it backwards somehow. There isn't any way *backward*, but there is a way forward. And just like that, the stairs reassume their original form and dimensions, and I am permitted to descend.

I decide: I'll just tell Regina what it's absolutely necessary to tell. Which isn't really all that much, come to think of it. Greer has certainly blown things out of proportion, sending me to Dr. Yaun. I'll tell Regina that. But I'll also say: "Maybe it's for the best." Talking to the doctor was actually sort of . . . fun, I'll say. That's not the right word, of course, but . . . well, it felt good— I'll say—just to say anything at all, then to sit in silence for a little while. And maybe, after all, it's time for me to be thinking about doing things a little differently, I'll say. Yes, that's the way to put it. I think this may be a wake-up call, I'll say. I need a change; I hope you understand.

But Regina is not in when I get home. I go into the kitchen to fix myself a sandwich, but I haven't even finished spreading the butter when I put down the knife, and return all the ingredients to the fridge. I go into the guest room and pull out my trainers from the back of the second closet—the one that's filled with winter jackets and old cassette tapes; the things we never use. I put on the trainers, a T-shirt, and a pair of old soccer shorts, which I've only ever used as pyjamas, and head outside. I don't even lock the door behind me when I go; I don't want to have to carry the keys.

At first I feel good. I mean, really good. And I'm surprised because I haven't been for a jog in—well, honestly, it must be about five years. It rained last night—quite a lot, actually; winter coming on. We'll get a few good downpours and for a month or two daytime temperatures will hover at around sixty degrees. There'll be a few nighttime frost warnings. By February it will be spring again, with highs in the eighties.

I head west, toward the river. I bet there's still water in it, though it hasn't rained since early morning. By suppertime it will have washed away, but there still should be some moving water now. I feel good and I can think of nothing better, nothing I'd rather be doing, than jogging down to the river to take a look at last night's rain. But then, before I even get to the underpass, I'm out of breath, and overheating, with this awful pain in my chest. It occurs to me that I'm having a heart attack, but then I remember. This is just how exercise feels.

I slow down, but not to a walk. I've got to be able to make it to the river, at least. If I make it to the river, I tell myself, I can stop. I'll walk back, I tell myself. Maybe even call a cab.

The underpass is cool and dark and I can hear the cars rushing overhead. On the other side, there's another highway. I find myself hoping there'll be a long line of traffic when I get there and I'll have to stop and wait—nobody ever stops at a crosswalk around here. But when I get to the highway there's not a single car in view: I have no choice but to keep going.

Now this is very definitely "the wrong side of the tracks." There's a couple of abandoned buildings and a chain-link fence surrounding an undeveloped double lot, functioning for the moment as a graveyard for used cars. A handwritten sign reads, Danny's Resurrection Auto, but there doesn't seem to be much resurrection going on. There's no one around, except for a couple of neglected-looking dogs who bark disinterestedly as I pass. Closer to the river there's a few family homes, with some more dogs in the yard. They race back and forth along the fence, yapping their heads off. I wonder what is going through their minds.

Now I'm really almost there. I can already see the turn, and from there it's just a short half block to the river. But now I see that a line of fire trucks is backed up all along the road, almost to the turn. When I get closer, I see a crowd of people gathered by the river, along with some TV crews. I slow my pace a little, though this means I'm probably not technically jogging any-more. I see two men in yellow slickers on the opposite side of the river. There are five or six ropes floating downstream of them and they're leaning their weight into them, bracing against the current, which is moving fast. When I reach the edge of the crowd, I stop. I'm breathing hard, and at first I just stand there, panting and looking around. I spot the woman from the doctor's office a little farther downriver. The one with the sunglasses and the red umbrella. Yes, it's definitely her. She's got her umbrella open, even though it hasn't rained in hours.

"Hey—" I say to the guy next to me. Like everyone else, he is looking straight ahead, without any readable expression. It feels a little odd at first to speak out loud, what with how quiet everyone is. "What's going on?"

The guy half turns, but he doesn't shift his eyes from the river. "They're looking for someone," he says. He has an accent. I don't know where from. "A body," he says.

Just as he says it, the orange ropes go taut and the men in the water sort of stagger. Then a stretcher is raised. And a body on the stretcher. It's one of those things that even when you're looking right at it you don't see straight. There's something sort of wobbly, uncertain . . . particularly about the body. It's no further away from me than the men in yellow slickers or the emergency vehicles with their lights flashing, but it looks different somehow. Sort of abstract; bloated, I guess, after sitting in the water for so long.

But then again, the river has risen only overnight.

I stand and watch as the body is lowered onto the opposite bank and the men in yellow slickers scramble out of the river. After that, the emergency team swoops in and there's nothing more to see. I stick around for a bit anyway. A lot of other people do, too, including the woman from the doctor's office, who I catch sight of from time to time—just her red umbrella bobbing up and down among the crowd.

I wonder if she's seen me, too—and if so, if she recognizes me. Or if anybody else does. I'm fairly incognito, dressed in soccer shorts and without my button-down shirt, but I glance around quickly—embarrassed, and for some reason ashamed.

It's tremendously unlikely, of course, that even if anyone did

notice me they would make a connection between myself and
the dead man, because . . . Well, because there isn't any. I tell
myself this again and again, but my heart is racing; it's a while
before I can calm myself down.

I try to train my attention on what is happening on the other
side of the river. I see the swarm of paramedics; they are moving quickly but somehow their motions appear too deliberate,
slow. They are lifting something into the back of the ambulance, but it's impossible to make out what. All I can see are the
yellow slickers, the flashing lights of the vehicles, the television
cameras trained on the scene.

Where's the body? I wonder. What have they done with the
body?

The sweat, which has drenched the front and back of my
T-shirt, has cooled, and suddenly I feel terribly cold.

THE OPENING

ONE DAY—LONG AFTER THE END OF THIS WORLD and into the beginning of the next—the director unlocked the gates to the first museum that had existed in nearly four thousand years, and the people streamed in.

It was a much better turnout than even she could have hoped—and she had been obliged from the start to be optimistic about the whole thing. Even when she had doubted the project, or her own involvement in it, she had done her best to hide it from everyone, including, whenever she reasonably could, from herself. One could not sink two marriages, all of one's time and energy, and a good deal of one's personal dignity into a single venture and not hope fervently it would come to *something* in the end. The night before the opening she had been particularly anxious, in large part due to the brief address she had been invited to deliver to the collection of archivists, historians, scholars, and local enthusiasts who had gathered in the museum foyer to help celebrate the occasion. She had sweated over the exact wording of her short speech for several weeks, rehearsing its "improvised" opening lines so many times and in so many various ways she began to suspect that when at last she opened her mouth she would be unable to utter anything at all.

When the time came, however, she had no choice but to smile through clenched teeth and bravely raise her glass.

"This," she began, "*this*" (here she gestured with both a practised, sweeping gaze and her still-raised glass around the vast, and mostly empty, hall) "is what we've been waiting for. For the past thirty-seven centuries. For seven major civilizations to rise and fall. Waiting, consciously or unconsciously during all of that time, for the eventual establishment of . . . this very museum."

A small laugh rippled through the audience; glasses, as well as a few appreciative voices, were raised. The director relaxed somewhat, drank, and allowed herself a brief, self-congratulatory smile. Then, bowing her head modestly, she continued from her notes.

"Because archival techniques have improved so dramatically, especially over the past several centuries," the director read, "there is—as many of you have already observed—a distinct contrast between the quality of some of the oldest artifacts in the museum and those that were able to benefit from more advanced methods of preservation. This should not" (here the director looked up sharply from her notes) "be understood as a shortcoming of the museum's collection, but just the opposite. I believe," she said, "that certain variations in the quality of the museum's artifacts will prove, in fact, to have valuable pedagogical applications, many of which we are not yet able to imagine. Not only will our visitors be able to consult a written record describing the approximate age and original location of each artifact, they will gain a tangible appreciation for the layers of time by *immediately apprehending them*. Where, that is," the director continued, "more recent acquisitions might well be indistinguishable in terms of their physical quality and condition from the familiar objects with which we surround ourselves daily, the older objects will appear . . . well" (the director looked up once more, and shrugged. She hoped desperately that, with her next word, she would hit the right note), "*old*."

She did. Once more, the audience laughed appreciatively. Relieved, the director continued, her voice—in proportion to her increased confidence—gaining energy and speed.

"It was nothing," she said, "quite honestly, that we would have consciously dreamed up. In fact, every effort was made to reduce, even eliminate altogether from the artifacts we recovered, *every trace* of the passage of time. But I strongly believe that future generations will thank us for preserving not only these historical objects themselves, but the very history of their preservation."

The audience applauded the director's address, and everyone agreed that—regardless of the turnout the next day, or any other, which was far from assured—the director and the other museum staff could feel frankly proud.

"This is not the kind of thing," said one attendee, for example, a few moments after the director had—raising her glass once more—concluded her remarks, "that is usually met with any sort of precisely measurable success—or, for that matter, failure. It's more of a . . . what would you call it?" She gave a short laugh. "I'd almost want," she said, removing a toothpicked meatball from a passing tray, "to use the word *faith*."

"Yes, isn't it ironic," a young archivist said, "that our job—of recording and preserving, so meticulously, the victories and failures of others—can, in itself, in no way be recorded or preserved? That we are left with nothing at all material in the end!"

"What's this?" asked a linguist standing nearby. "Nothing material? Look around, my dear boy!"

The linguist's words echoed loudly through the hall. It had been kept largely empty with the aim of offering the visitor, upon exit and entry, some—much needed—space for reflection. Only a few choice artifacts stood along the back walls at thoughtfully spaced intervals, gesturing in a general way to the rise and fall of at least several long-expired civilizations. Now there was a brief pause as everyone, heeding the linguist's advice, looked around. After a few moments, their gazes had travelled (just as the museum's architect had hoped) through the wide front windows toward the museum gates: two large—overwhelmingly material—towers in a state of semi-collapse, each having been carefully reconstructed in order to evoke its "original" state of demolition.

Someone laughed. "Well, quite right," she said, proffering her glass to a passing waiter, who obediently filled it. "If it is not as obvious to our visitors tomorrow as it is to us tonight, then—" She took a swallow of wine.

"Blast it all!" someone else said, raising his own glass in the air.

"Yes, blast it all!" one or two others said, and everyone drank to that.

By the time the doors actually opened the next day, the line had snaked its way down the street and turned the first corner— a distance (as one of the ticket collectors noted) of nearly a quarter mile.

The director could disguise neither her surprise nor her excitement. "Now, this," she exclaimed as she paced between the ticket counters and the museum office where, in fifteen-minute intervals, she recorded the increase in ticket sales, "this is what we were waiting for!"

The people poured in. From nine o'clock sharp, when the director ceremoniously turned the key, there was a steady flow of visitors through the museum gates. They turned in circles in the great hall—abstractedly folding the corners of their museum maps—before gradually turning their attention to the thoughtfully spaced objects that lined the back wall. Finally, they drifted off into the adjacent hall, where glass cabinets displayed the souvenirs of forgotten civilizations. Items had been organized not according to age or origin but according to "utility" and "theme." In one display cabinet, for example, visitors observed every writing implement that had been used over the past thirty-seven centuries; in another, every personal weapon. Examples of the visual and plastic arts from various epochs were presented in a series of long corridors connecting the main cabinet rooms to the great hall, and adjacent to these was a theatre where examples of film and television from several key periods in the history of cinema played on a continuous reel. On the second level, a reproduction shopping mall had been designed, each section reflecting a different consumer trend, beginning in the nineteenth and following through to the end of the twenty-sixth century. On the third level, there were more cabinet rooms, and an interactive display on various stages in the development of telecommunications.

It was not long before the visitors became weary. Where at first they had read the long and detailed descriptions that accompanied each cabinet, they were, as the hours passed, no longer able to distinguish between the various epochs, or the themes according to which each carefully curated item had been—by the director, her well-intentioned staff, and a stream of devoted interns—meticulously arranged.

This confusion had been foreseen, even invited, by the director and her staff. After all—as the director had often remarked—it was only natural, and not at all counter to the museum's overall aim, that in looking back over the course of thirty-seven centuries the line between them should begin to blur slightly; that visitors should begin to feel the bewildering sensation of several civilizations rising and falling together—of all of history occurring at once.

If this was indeed the aim of the museum, its opening was a great success. Before long, the visitors began to wander the halls as though through a dream. They no longer read the carefully worded descriptions posted beside each object, but began instead to "sense" the difference between the objects that surrounded them, to feel time in layers. They found the newer items, for example, disconcertingly familiar. The older items appeared, and "felt," by contrast, old. After a while, they lost touch with even these differences, and all the artifacts, regardless of their stated or apparent age, began to look as though they had all been used at the same time in history and for the same purpose. Visitors began to find themselves in rooms they had already travelled through and not recognize the artifacts there, or, equally, they would wander into a wing of the museum they hadn't known existed and believe they were merely retracing their steps.

It was in precisely this sort of bewildered state that three young visitors, a man and a woman somewhere between the ages of twenty and twenty-five, and a boy who could have been no older than seventeen, stumbled upon an unmarked door in the museum's upper west wing. The door opened off the back of a hollowed metal shell—or seemed to. When the young man approached and tried to turn the door's handle it felt loose, as though there was nothing for it to catch upon.

The shell itself had been classified variously over the years. Several experts had suggested, for instance, that it had once served as the interior dome of a cathedral, whereas others insisted it had been a fibreglass swimming pool mould, and still others maintained it was a fragment from a twenty-first-century nuclear bomb. This was all recorded on a posted sign outside the entrance to the shell—and was ignored equally by all three young visitors as they entered, making their way to the opposite wall.

Once again, the young man jiggled the door's handle, and once again there seemed nothing for it to catch upon inside. Bored, he gave it one last shake, turned—was just about to go—when something clicked. The young man glanced back at his companions, surprised. Then, as if acting on instinct, he leaned his weight against the heavy door. Beneath him, he felt it shift. Ever so slightly. It was clear that the door had not been opened for a very long time.

Now the young woman and the boy approached and leaned their weights against the door as well. All three pushed as hard as they could—until the door's edge was framed with silver light and, at last, it swung open.

They stood together, then, blinking against a sudden brightness.

At first they were unsure what they were looking at—or if they were looking at anything at all.

But then . . .

Sky, the young woman thought to herself as she took a step toward the light. She did not know where the word had come from. She could not remember ever having learned it, or even having heard it spoken.

Perhaps she had, though. Perhaps she had heard it in some long-forgotten History of Science class, or read it on one of the museum signs, before she had given up reading them several hours before.

She just, suddenly, knew. And, propelled by this knowledge— or memory, or desire, or whatever it was—rather than by any conscious decision, she took another step forward. As she crossed the threshold, however, she stopped, choking suddenly on a sharp blast of unfiltered air. She looked back and saw that her companions had followed. That they, too, had stopped and were now bent double, choking and gasping on air.

Was this, she wondered, the last room in the museum . . . or was it . . . was it possible?

Something flickered overhead. She looked up. A pale, nearly colourless shape drifted across what otherwise seemed a limitless stretch of open sky; below, the same shape appeared in the negative, sweeping its way, in a dark swath, across the earth.

She had never seen a shadow before. Her parents had never seen a shadow. Perhaps her grandparents had. Perhaps something like a shadow still flickered in the sound of their voices when they spoke of the past. But she herself had never once seen a shadow. And yet, here it was, and somehow . . . she knew. She recognized the flickering patterns of light and shade, the way that one moment everything appeared bright and clear and the next moment was plunged in sudden darkness.

As first her eyes adjusted to the light, and then, more slowly, as her lungs adjusted to the unfiltered air, she was able to observe things more closely. To notice and recognize what had so far escaped her.

Grass. Water. Flowers. Trees.

And still, she did not know how she knew the names of the things she saw, or if what was awakening within her was a deep memory, or a longing for something she had not yet known. Still, she did not know if she had stumbled into the last—best— room of the museum, or if somehow she had managed to leave the museum entirely, and with it the known world.

But if the museum director could have seen her and her companions then—if she had not, that is, been kept so busy running back and forth between the main foyer and the museum office in order to record, in fifteen-minute intervals, the steady increase in ticket sales—she would have been very pleased, indeed, to see her visitors as they turned in circles and looked and gaped and wondered at what they saw, and were unable, in their vast confusion, to detect the difference any longer between the last century of the old world and the first century of the next.

A HORSE,
A VINE

O unhappy citizens, what madness? Do you think the enemy's sailed away?

Virgil, *The Aeneid*, Book II

I KNEW THAT I COULD COUNT ON DEAN. He was like a brother to me, but better than that. Ever since we'd met on our first day of Basic, both of us just eighteen years old. Turned out we'd both grown up near Houston. Dean was from just north of Sugar Land, in Mission Bend, and I was from Alvin; in good traffic, just a little less than an hour away. Maybe it was that. Whatever it was, we understood each other—which is saying something. Dean is not a guy who is easily understood. He's always been nuts. Even in Basic. He started picking up odd jobs even then, "just to keep things interesting." Mostly it was nothing. Just roughing up a guy in town every now and then, for a friend. But after a while he got into some real dirty work, too. I kept telling him he was going to get himself into trouble but he'd just say, nah, and when he did get into trouble it didn't have anything to do with any of that shit. He was always pretty good about it—didn't leave a lot of loose ends.

What happened was he got called in for a domestic on account of this girl, Natalie, who he wasn't even serious about. They issued him with protective orders, but that suited him just fine, and for a while it looked like they were going to let it go at that. But then, a year later, when his term of service was up, he was denied re-enlistment. If you ask me, it didn't have anything to do with the girl, though that's what they said. Everyone could just sort of tell that Dean was a little—unhinged.

———

Dean pretty near lost his mind when he heard about it. You can imagine. That was the beginning of September, 2001. I was home on leave—and I was the first person he called. I told him, Come on back home, we'll get you sorted out. And so he came back and calmed down a little. He even managed to pick up a few jobs, but his heart wasn't in it. He'd come over to visit Tracy and me all the time. We'd drink beer and play video games until three or four in the morning and we'd both fall asleep in the living room, one of us in the La-Z-Boy and the other stretched out on the couch. The night before the Twin Towers fell was a night like that. We'd been playing *Colony Wars* but hadn't even managed to finish the game. When we woke up Dean said we should finish it out because he'd been winning. I agreed—but only because I still had a chance. It's a good game that way, more like real life. Even if you lose a few battles you can still win the overall—it's just about how everything balances out. Also, it's not like most games where it's either you win or you die. There are five different endings to the game: two of them good and three of them bad. So that's like real life, too. There's always a chance that things will work out—but more of a chance that they won't.

I was trying to concentrate on the game because I was still losing when Tracy came in with Cody screaming on her hip—he was still just tiny then. She just sort of stood there at first, looking at us. Letting Cody cry like that. Even if she had tried to say something, though, I probably wouldn't have heard her because of how much noise Cody was making and because I was still trying to concentrate—finish the game, even if I was losing—and because Dean was yelling at me the whole time, too, saying, You're gonna die, motherfucker! You are *so* going to die!

Finally Tracy walked over, the kid still screaming, and flicked the screen over to the TV, and just at the moment that she clicked over—the first tower fell. It was fucked up. I didn't even know what was happening at first. Like it was sort of a joke. Or a clip from a movie or something. Dean said, *Damn!* in the same way he did when I beat the shit out of him playing *Blast Radius* or *Hogs of War*.

After that Dean had a job. He got hired on at Blackwater, and he liked it a lot better anyway than he liked the marines. He told me I should get discharged and join up, but I didn't think so. I'd just got back from a six-month tour in Afghanistan and didn't want to go back anymore if I could help it. I wanted to get transferred to the Northern Command. Get posted at Fort Sam, maybe—be closer to Tracy and Cody that way. Plus, I liked the idea of homeland defence. It was an arithmetic thing. Say you blew up three guys over there in Iraq or Afghanistan—you never could be certain if they were the right guys. At home, if anybody tried anything, you'd know for sure when you blew them up that you were getting the right guy. If any more 9/11 shit was going to happen, I liked the idea of being right here, waiting. Couldn't stand the thought of being stuck sitting on my thumbs over at Camp Eggers or Fiddler's Green.

What, you getting spooked or something? Dean said when I told him about the homeland defence thing.

I shook my head. Nah.

Soft? he said. He poked me in the gut.

I shook my head again. You can see for yourself, I said. No.

The way I said it that time, he left me alone. But the next time I saw him, he brought it up again.

Still spooked? he asked. I said I'd told him before that I wasn't.

It's all right, he said. Everybody gets it sometime. But you got to remember—it's not just about killing and getting killed. You're an artist, he told me. A warrior. Don't forget that. Then he took this book from his pocket and read me something out of it that he said had been written by a Roman general something like two thousand years ago.

For someone who came across like such a special needs case most of the time, Dean was actually pretty deep. He used to carry *The Art of War* around with him in Basic. Now it was *Meditations*, by Marcus Aurelius.

We were having beers at the Triple Crown in Mission Bend, and when he got up to pay he shoved the book across the table toward me. Take it, he said. You might learn something. Then he made a face as if to say bigger miracles have happened, slammed a tip down on the table, and headed toward the door.

I liked the book. It made you think about things. I liked the way it was written, too, in these short little sentences, sort of like the psalms in the Bible. When I didn't understand them, I would just skip ahead, and it didn't matter. But most of the time I understood, and it was pretty cool to know that someone else was wondering about all the shit I was wondering about even two thousand years ago. Even though it made me a bit sad to realize that meant nobody had figured anything out in all of that time. Like this one part, where he says that everything exists for some reason. Even a horse, he says, or a vine—so why do you even have to wonder about it? But when he says it like that, it's obvious he's wondered himself or else he wouldn't have had to ask about why. And then he says, *Even the sun will say, I am for some purpose, and the rest of the gods will say the same. For what purpose then art thou?*

I liked that. I'd even sort of repeat it to myself sometimes. *For what purpose then art thou?* Because even though it sounded like a question, it was sort of an answer, too.

Then, a week or so later, just before I was due to ship out, Dean showed up at my house with a copy of *RifleShooter* magazine.

This will make you feel better, he said.

I feel fine, I said.

No, seriously, he said. Check it out. If you get blown up over there I'll do this for you—promise. And if I get blown up, you can do it for me.

He flipped open the magazine from the back and read from an advertisement in the classified section.

How about honoring your deceased loved one, he read, pulling a face, *by sharing with him or her one more round of clay targets, one last bird hunt, one last stalk hunt—*

I interrupted. Is this for real? I said.

Ha ha! Dean said. Hell yeah. Then continued to read the ad out loud. Only this time he stayed deadly serious.

All you had to do, according to this ad, was send these guys some ashes and they'd turn it into live ammunition for you.

One pound of ash was enough for roughly 250 shells, they said. They even did mantelpiece carriers and engraved nameplates.

What better way, Dean read, *to be remembered. Now you can have the peace of mind that you can continue to protect your home and family even after you are gone.*

That's the part that got me. I realized sort of all of a sudden what had been bothering me ever since I got back from my first tour. It wasn't that I was scared of dying. The thing that rattled me was thinking about what would happen *after* I died. Not to me, but to Tracy and Cody. I'd start thinking about it, all the crazy shit that could happen, and it would drive me nuts, because there's no end to the possibilities that can happen after you're dead—even more than can happen when you're alive, and that is pretty much anything. I would get so crazy sometimes thinking about this that it got so I couldn't even hardly breathe. I'd get this feeling in my gut like someone had just stuck me with an icepick, and after that I couldn't breathe or think straight anymore. I'd just have to stand there with that pain in my gut until it passed. Sometimes it would last for a good couple of minutes, which is a long time to go without breathing. It wouldn't happen all the time, but I could never tell when it was going to.

After I got back from my second tour it was even worse. I didn't even have to be thinking about anything and it would happen. I'd be sitting there playing a video game with Cody or eating a sandwich at the kitchen table or Tracy and I would be fucking, and I'd feel it. A sharp pain in my gut first, and then my lungs starting to shut down. I'd try to shake it, but there wasn't anything I could do. It got so bad I had to tell Tracy. It wasn't like she didn't notice. You can't freeze up like that on someone when you're in the middle of fucking them and not have them notice.

She told me not to worry. Nothing was going to happen, she said. But even if it did, I shouldn't worry, because she could take care of herself, and Cody, too—and I knew it. She was used to it, she said, what with me being gone all the time. And she was right—I knew. That's the thing. It was weird. If I thought about it I knew that I was lucky that way. Tracy was tough, and she was smart, too. We kept a gun in the house, and she knew how to use it. She was even a pretty good shot, and wasn't someone who was likely to lose it and not know how to aim right, or be afraid to shoot if she needed to. I could pretty much count on that. She would get this look on her face when she was serious about something and you knew that no one was ever going to mess with her.

Like that time when she came into the room and switched on the TV and the tower fell. Or the time that Cody, when he was real little, nearly choked and died—and probably would have, too, if she hadn't been around to save him. It still makes me sick to think about that, because it was my fault it happened. I was feeding him, and I guess I hadn't cut the pieces up small enough—I figured they were pretty small already. But then Cody got quiet and his eyes got this real scared look to them, like they were going to pop out of his head. It was fucked up because it wasn't even like he choked or anything first. He just stayed quiet and then got even quieter and then his eyes were popping out of his head. I bolted for the phone and yelled for Tracy, but then before I could get to the phone even, Tracy was there, walking by me like she didn't even see me—that look on her face. She went straight for the kid, turned him upside down, and started thumping him on the back, hard, until pretty soon the little piece of chicken that had got stuck in his throat shot out of his mouth, and he was crying and puking all over the floor.

You useless piece of shit, Tracy said, without looking at me. By the time anyone got around to coming over here in an ambulance it would have been too late. Don't you know that? Then she scooped up Cody and took him off to the bathroom to get him cleaned up.

The piece of chicken had flown clear across the room and landed right beside my foot. I remember that after she left, and took the kid, I just sat down on the floor next to it and looked at it, and thought about how small it was, and how you never knew what it was that was going to fuck you. How you had to be prepared for every little thing.

After my third tour I had that pain in my gut all the time. It was funny, because it didn't happen to me in the field. Over there, I felt strong and I didn't give a shit. A lot of guys get scared. If they've seen combat, or had any close calls, they start to feel like everything they see is going to jump up and bite them. But I wasn't like that. See, I wasn't afraid of dying—it wasn't that. It was everything else. When I was home I would start to feel it all over again. I couldn't help it. I'd start thinking about how everything was all connected. I mean, how every little thing that happened would set off something else happening. And how that would set off something else, and that if

I died there was nothing I could do to stop all the shit that my dying would set off in the world without knowing, ahead of time, what it would be.

I started thinking more about that ad Dean had read. I thought about how funny it would be to be sitting up on the shelf. Just ready and waiting up there for shit to happen. To be hard and cold as metal, all loaded and ready inside Tracy's Taurus 1911, which I had got her, and which she knew how to use. I started thinking about it all the time. How it would feel to be inside that gun, with her hand on the trigger. But then when I really did have her hands on me I would get that icepick feeling again and if she was on top of me I'd have to push her off because I couldn't breathe. It got to be pretty bad that way, because she would get hurt like maybe I didn't love her anymore, or didn't think she was sexy, and I would tell her, no, that wasn't it, it was just this thing that I couldn't explain and it didn't have anything to do with her—not really. But women always think that everything is about them and so she would turn over and cry and say, for the fifth time, Don't you think I'm sexy, or what? And I would tell her again how she was the sexiest woman in the world, and that she should know that. I knew she did. Everywhere we went people were always checking her out and I knew that she noticed. That she liked it, even.

Who wouldn't?

Most of the time, I didn't mind. Sometimes, though—especially when we went to Galveston Island, where her best friend Anelise Hutson's brother, Brian, had a place—I did. She would wear this tiny little bikini, show off, and everyone would look at her—including Brian. There was just something about that guy—the way that he looked at her—that gave me the creeps. I don't know why because it wasn't like I was jealous. I had no reason to be. He was just this skinny dude with a paunch who didn't do anything all day except sit out on his front porch and answer the phone. Seriously. He owned a Sea-Doo rental place just outside of town, and then his house was a few miles past that, but he hardly ever went into the store. He had these young guys working for him there, so I guess he didn't need to. Instead, he would sit around at home all day answering his phone. The way he talked about it, it was as if the Sea-Doo rental business was the most important thing on the face of the planet. The ringer on his phone was never turned on—it would just vibrate in his pocket and every time it vibrated he'd jump up and, real exaggerated, mouth out "Sorry," then take the call. It was so fucking stupid. He'd actually mouth the word, even before he'd picked up the phone.

Except for that, though, I liked the beach. And we were lucky to know someone who had a house literally right on the water. The house was stuck up on stilts and sometimes after it stormed or when the tide came in high, the water would rush right up under the deck. I liked sitting out there. Tracy was right—it helped me relax. We'd take chairs and put them in the shallow water and drink beer with our feet stuck in the sand. I'd build sandcastles with Cody and then help knock them down, or take a magazine down with me and stick my nose in it so I didn't have to pretend to care about whatever Brian was saying. He was always saying stupid shit to Anelise and Tracy whenever he wasn't saying it into the phone.

But when I came back after my third tour it was winter and

so we didn't go to the beach, and I didn't relax. Tracy kept bugging me to see a shrink, but I told her it wasn't that sort of a thing.

Well what sort of a thing is it? she wanted to know.

I was pretty sure she had told her friends about me by then—about how we weren't even really sleeping together anymore. I just sort of felt it. You know, like when we'd be hanging out with Anelise, I could feel that she knew. Maybe even Brian knew. It made me sick to think about that, and so finally I agreed. I got an appointment with a shrink at Fort Sam and drove up the next day.

It was a lady shrink—a blonde. Her hair was done up real complicated on the top of her head and sprayed into place. It didn't even look real. For an hour, I sat in her office and she smiled at me and nodded and whatever I said she wrote down in this little notebook she had. It was all pretty normal, she said, everything I was saying. I said, This isn't any PTSD shit, if that's what you're thinking. I know how I am and I do not even give a shit when I am out there, so it's not that. And she nodded and said that was normal, too.

I started to hate her. The way she sat there, smiling and nodding, and how when she nodded not one single hair moved out of place on her head. I figured that all that attention to her hair was probably intended to distract from the fact that she was overweight, and not that attractive overall. After she was done with me she was probably going to drive over to Kroger's to stock up on diet foods. She was probably thinking about that right now. I started to get mad, thinking about it myself. Why was it always fat people who dieted? Why didn't they ever get thin?

Tracy could eat anything she wanted. Even when she was pregnant, she didn't get fat—not even a little bit. It wasn't that I cared about it one way or the other, this shrink being fat or not. It just showed a lack of resolve. That was the problem with the whole goddamn country. Sitting there in the shrink's office, it started to become very clear. Nobody really gave a shit. They said they did, but they didn't. Everyone was just sitting around, getting fat and soft and not giving a shit, while all the while—guess what? Everyone else was getting mean and hard.

While I was thinking about this, the shrink was setting up a video game on her big-screen TV and telling me how to work the functions on the control pad she'd given me like I'd never played a video game before in my life. The game was pretty much the same as the ones we'd used in Basic, actually—except a lot cheaper. You know how I could tell? There weren't any shadows. You need shadows to make things look real. The cheap games don't bother.

So I take the control from the shrink and I'm wandering around, blowing shit up, and every time I detonate she's saying, *How does this make you feel?* And I'm saying, Like this is a cheap piece of shit. My kid still buys the fucking Easter bunny and he wouldn't buy this.

And that's when it hit me. What's wrong with me. How come every time I come home this weird shit starts happening. There's no fucking shadows! You go to Kroger's—or to Target, or the mall, or the fucking dentist office. You stay home even, in your own house, with the fluorescent light in the kitchen and the blinds closed to save on air conditioning. There weren't any shadows anywhere!

I started to get freaked out then, thinking about it. Like maybe nothing was even fucking real, and I just got up, the shrink still smiling and nodding, and went home. Tracy was there. She said, How did it go? But I didn't say anything.

I went into the kitchen instead. I was right. There was not one fucking shadow. Tracy followed me in there, but I turned around and headed into the TV room, where Cody was sitting on the couch playing *Darksiders*. I sat down beside him and started to watch. The game is actually pretty boring, but it's all right for a kid. You play one of the Four Horsemen of the Apocalypse and have to try to balance the forces of heaven and hell. If you're lucky, you make it to Endwar and you get to punish anyone who's still stuck on Earth. The kid was doing okay, but I didn't think he was going to make it to Endwar. Pretty soon Tracy came in and stood right in front of the screen. She had one hip stuck out, like she wanted to start something. The kid kept playing. He had to lean around sideways so he could see around her legs.

You're not even trying, she said.

Get out of the way, I said. The kid can't see.

She kept standing there. That look on her face.

That's when I lost it. I don't even know what I said. I didn't care half the time because I was thinking, It *doesn't even matter, this isn't even fucking real*. But then all of a sudden it was. Tracy was grabbing Cody up from the couch and stuffing his arms into his jacket. It was January and it was pretty cold outside. She was saying, Fuck you, you know that? Fuck you. I'm sick of this shit. Then she put on her own coat, grabbed her car keys off the little hook by the door, and was gone.

———

She didn't come home that night, or the next. I kept waiting for her, you know. Like an idiot. Expecting her—every moment. But she didn't come. I stayed inside, with the blinds drawn, and I waited. I tried to read some *Meditations* but I couldn't keep the words straight on the page. Nothing made any sense. I played *Darksiders* because it was still in the PlayStation and I couldn't be bothered to change the game, but I kept winning. It wasn't even fun anymore.

When Tracy didn't come home by eight o'clock on Sunday, I called her mom's place. I was angry by then, and had just started to say something like, This is fucked, she can't steal the kid, when Tracy's mom said she hadn't seen her and didn't know a thing about it. I was about to call Anelise when . . . I didn't need to anymore.

I don't know how I knew, but I did. I jumped in the car and I drove all the way to Galveston. It took me just a little less than twenty minutes. Usually it takes half an hour or more, depending on traffic, but I was driving pretty fast.

I didn't slow down till I was past Galveston. I thought at first maybe I wouldn't recognize the street, but I recognized it all right. I turned in and drove just far enough so I could see the drive, and sure enough there was Tracy's car parked right out front. Even though I already knew I would find it there, it still felt pretty bad when I did. It felt so bad that I got out of the car and puked in the culvert. Then I got back in, turned the car around, and started driving again. I was shaking all over. I thought I should pull over I was shaking so bad, but I kept driving. I drove all the way into town, shaking like that, then I pulled over on the seawall and ordered a beer at this one place where I could sit outside. No one else was out there, it was too cold, but I sat out there for a long time, and just looked out across the highway to where the ocean stretched out, flat and hard looking, in all directions. It was sort of hard to tell where it ended and the sky began, and I could see the rigs out there and because it was just starting to get dark their lights were shining so that it looked like they were the first stars. I made a wish on one of them—just like I always had Cody do whenever I was with him and we saw the first star come into the sky for real. I wished that I was a bullet, and that I was at that very moment coursing through Brian Hutson's body. That I was that hard and sharp and dark and that I was just then being slowed, only very slightly, by Brian Hutson's cranial bone; just then being splashed with spinal fluid as I severed the connective tissue between his skull and the soft tissue of his brain; just then interrupting the information travelling between his nervous system and his heart.

I sat there for a long time, wishing that. By then it had got dark and real stars had come out in the sky. I realized I was chilled to the bone, that I had only drunk half of my beer, and that the kid that was serving me was looking at me funny. I got up and paid and drove back home and all the time I was thinking hard.

I already had a pretty good plan, but I wanted to be extra-certain because after you're dead it's even harder to make sure that things go according to plan than when you are not. Dean was going to be back in town in a few days, and I was glad about that. I knew I could count on him to help me think the whole thing through again—then to carry it out.

The first thing I needed to do was place my order with the company in Alabama. I'd order fifty shotshells for Dean's Smith and Wesson and two hundred for Tracy's Taurus. I wanted to make sure she'd have plenty left over after I was gone. I'd arrange for it all in my will, so there wouldn't be any mistake. Make sure that the shells—when they were ready—would be sent to Dean's address in Mission Bend, and not to Tracy. That way he could go to Brian's house and shoot off thirty or so rounds into Brian's body before delivering the rest of the ACPs to Tracy so she could put some in her Taurus—and still have plenty left to put up on the shelf.

The more I thought about it, the more certain I was I could carry it off. It was really very simple, I thought. The plan pretty much foolproof. After I was dead, Dean would call Brian and tell him who he was. Nothing but the truth: he was a friend of mine; had something to personally deliver, on my behalf. It was my parting wish—some bullshit like that. You could pretty much guarantee that a guy like Brian wouldn't say no.

If Dean waited awhile—a couple of weeks, maybe—then arrived on a weekday, any time before six, I figured chances were pretty good that Tracy would be back at work and Cody would be at his grandmother's house, like usual. Dean could chit-chat with Brian a bit, and then—before he got into any of the really dirty business—get him to empty the safe, which I knew for a fact he kept upstairs. That way it would be Brian and not me that would end up compensating Dean for his trouble. All of my insurance money would go to Tracy instead.

The only real risk that I could foresee was if anyone happened to be around when Dean arrived at the house, but I figured the chances of it were pretty slim and that, if Dean didn't feel right about it—and especially if Tracy's car was there—he could always just turn around and come back another time. Or call up on his cell and tell Brian he was running late or something, then just wait around until the coast was clear. I could just picture him. Pulled off on the side of the road out there, chanting Sun Tzu or some shit.

But Brian didn't have many friends, and that time of year those roads off the main highway were pretty desolate, especially during the week, so I didn't think he'd need to bother. No one would hear the shots and no one would see him either come or go. There was always the possibility that something else could go wrong, of course—something that I wasn't thinking of, and couldn't foresee—but the more I thought about it the more clear it became to me that you had to take certain risks in death, just like in life, and that now all I had to do was wait.

Even just thinking about it, now—inside my own house, with the lights on and the blinds closed—I start to feel it. It's like I'm already hurtling at 3200 feet per second to lodge myself behind an ear. To enter at the throat, the belly, the knee, the heart. If Dean discharges thirty bullets into Brian Hutson's body, roughly 0.2 ounces of my own body will be left inside his. This is not a lot when you think about it, but sometimes it's the smallest things—the things you least suspect—that turn out to matter the most.

It's the details, see, the shadows, that make a thing real, and the moment that Brian Hutson feels the first bullet lodge in his chest—or even in the split-second flash right before it hits—he will know this, too. He will feel, for the first time in his life, how everything has a purpose.

How brief it will all be—yet how final. I wait for Dean to show up, and I think about that. About how at the very end there will just be that question. *For what purpose then art thou?* About how, for a single, unmeasurable moment as I whistle through Brian Hutson's body, I will *be* with that question.

Before—in another moment, still less measurable than the first—he will respond to that question with a question of his own. A question that will seem, for that briefest of moments, like an answer. Before all questions are finally extinguished. As it is the nature of questions—and all things—to be.

THE VISIT

THE DOOR IS OPEN. The small boy leans his weight into it, and enters, the tall boy behind him. A breeze sweeps across the room as the boys enter, without—somehow—disturbing any air.

The room is not clean, and the outside air is no match for the smell—which is really more like an object than a smell. Though not like an object that can be easily removed.

Maybe this is because it smells like every other cheap hotel that ever existed. Because it gives you the distinct impression that even if you managed to remove the smell from this particular room, it would only be the beginning of all the rooms and all the smells that exist, and will always exist, in rooms just like this one.

—What is it exactly?

Years of tobacco, inexpensive food, and—in equal parts— sex and loneliness suffused into the carpet and the ceiling tiles.

—At what point did it fix itself permanently there? By what process of slow accretion did it collect, and in what moment did it become inevitable that it could not be scrubbed out?

These are the great mysteries; the boys do not contemplate them. They push their way steadily into the middle of the room.

It is empty. Or appears to be. Just the breeze blows through, stirring in the dank air, which has never been stirred, only the idea of movement.

The small boy looks at the tall boy; the tall boy looks back.

What is the point of an open door, their looks seem to ask, if there is nothing to open upon?

The small boy is about to turn, assuming the tall boy will follow, when a noise startles them.

They turn.

There is a third in the room. A man. Sitting slouched so low in his chair that all the boys are able to see are two thin legs and the slanted brim of a hat. This is evidently why the man was not immediately observable to them—although now that he is, neither boy can understand how they failed to notice him before. His legs stick out well past the frame of his chair—not to mention the brim of his hat. How the boys had seen both the legs and the hat without connecting them to the idea of a man is a question that, for the briefest of moments, puzzles them both.

But then they forget the question and the man becomes a man. Now it is as if he had never been a pair of legs disconnected from the idea of a man, or no man at all, because they had failed to recognize him.

As soon as he becomes a man, he rises to greet them.

—If they had never recognized him, would he have continued to sit, disconnected even from the idea of himself? Never to raise himself, if shakily, on thin legs, to greet them?

The boys do not contemplate this, or any other thing.

The man has risen. Shakily, on thin legs. He extends his hand. He is glad to see them.

When he speaks, his voice is rough and old, as though he has never spoken.

The tall boy does not accept the man's hand, however, and

the small boy does not accept it either. Pretty soon the hand is withdrawn.

When he sits down again he is facing the two boys.

There is not much to say.

The small boy fetches a glass from the cupboard.

So there is a little kitchenette in the corner, and the boy is already there, fetching the glass. The glass is ringed on the inside like the high-water mark on a dock or a quay. The small boy runs the glass under the tap and attempts to scrub the ring from the inside of the glass. It does not come off easily.

He fixes a drink and drops a few pieces of ice in the glass. He brings the drink to the man.

All the while, the man is speaking to the tall boy, who is relieved when the small boy returns and hands the man the glass. If the man takes a drink he will be required to pause. He will not be able to say anything for a little while.

—What has the man been speaking about all this time? What could he possibly have to say to the tall boy—or to anyone?

The man takes the drink. His hand is not steady, but it is steadier now that he holds the glass in his hand. He puts one thin leg over the other and takes a sip from the glass. He takes only one sip, but he swallows twice.

—How long has the man been in the room before anyone entered and recognized him there?

Evidently, it has been quite a long time. It is difficult, in any case, to imagine that he has ever left the room, and the boys do not. It is enough to say that he has always existed in that room. Just as the smell has always been suffused in the carpet and in the ceiling tile.

The man begins to speak again, but his words are slurred, and what he says makes little sense. Is it, the small boy wonders, not knowing what the man has said before or not knowing what he will say next that makes it so difficult to understand what he is saying now?

The more the small boy thinks about it, the more confused he gets, until finally he is no longer able to discern the difference between not making sense and failing to understand.

In either case, he does not understand. He realizes this and, abruptly, the man stops talking—his last sentence left dangling in midair. He lurches forward as though his drink has been knocked from his hand and he is trying to catch it before it falls. But the drink has not been knocked, and only his own action threatens to spill the contents of the glass.

The ice rattles in the drink, startling both himself and the boys.

"Wait," the man says. He looks at each of the boys in turn.

Who are you? his look seems to say.

The boys blink, and do not answer the question that has not been asked.

The man's eyes are very blue and marked at the edges with small pink veins. The veins are like the crooked maps of rivers that spread their way from the eye's dark centre toward its unmapped edges—toward what is literally unseen.

The man looks at the glass as if noticing it in his hand for the first time. He puts it down. Then he looks around the room as though noticing it, and everything in it, for the first time. The print on the wall above the bed. The dark water stain on the ceiling tile, which, though it appears to belong to the room in a fundamental rather than a merely circumstantial way, must have appeared slowly over time—as generations of hotel guests alternatively cleansed and drowned themselves in the leaking faucets and undrainable bathtubs of the upper floors.

If the man could relieve himself of these and the other objects in the room as easily as he put down the glass, he would. He looks at the ceiling again and now he is quite certain that the mark he sees is not a trace, a stain, accrued slowly over time, but instead an expression of the room as it is, and will be, and has always been.

Yes, for a moment he is quite certain: everything is as it is and will be and always has been. And yet . . .

If this is so, the room should at least seem familiar, he thinks. In fact, he cannot ever remember having entered it, and is now surprised to find himself inside. He is surprised to look down at his body and find his own thin legs beneath him. Surprised to see his hands shaking slightly at the end of his arms—ever since, having set down the glass, he's had nothing to hold.

The small boy shifts uncomfortably. He looks in the direction of the tall boy, and the tall boy looks back.

Again, the man lurches forward in his chair as though his glass has been knocked from his hand, but now he isn't even holding on to anything. The glass is on the table beside him and there is nothing to spill. Still, the man lurches forward as though the glass has been knocked—then he steadies himself again.

"I know who you are," he says, looking back and forth between the boys.

The boys shake their heads, no. But the man gets up. He stands unsteadily.

"Give him something to drink," the tall boy says. He takes a step forward, touches the man on the shoulder, tries to settle him again in his chair.

The small boy picks up the drink the man has set down and offers it to the man. The man looks at him, then at the drink extended in the small boy's hand.

"I know you," the man says.

"Have something to drink," says the tall boy.

The man looks at the tall boy, then again at the drink in the small boy's hands.

It is, very briefly, possible that the man will not take it. That he will instead hit it angrily out of the small boy's hand. For a moment, anything is possible. But then the moment passes and the man takes the drink. He sits down, laughs, then drains the glass.

"Yes, I know you," the man says again, when the glass is empty. "I know why you've come."

He tries to explain, but the boys are not listening. They can't wait to get out of the room now, to go back the way they came. They catch only a few words the old man says—words that, on their own, make very little sense, because they've missed everything in between.

But it is not only that. By now it is clear that even if the boys had been properly listening, everything would still be missing. The man continues to speak, but he is not making sense. Even he understands that now.

The boys move slowly in the direction of the open door. If the man notices, he does not let on; he continues to speak.

The boys edge their way backward, one small step at a time. They do not want to startle the man. They do not want to appear to be leaving too soon.

They wish desperately that the man would stop talking; that the man would drink quickly; that they had never entered the room.

The small boy reaches the kitchen, takes a bag of ice from the fridge, and empties it onto the floor. The tall boy picks up a can of soda from the counter and pours it on the ice, between himself and the man.

The carpet darkens. The waning light, streaming in from the window at the end of the room, glints off the ice that's been scattered on the floor.

The man watches as the boys retreat. He does not appear to be surprised. His eyes are pale at the edges, though, as if they are suddenly seeing farther—and you can see he is afraid.

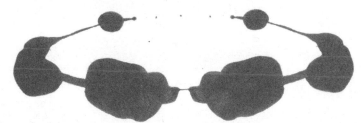

THE LAST FRONTIER

SABRINA LOWE-MACKEY WAS STILL IN HIGH SCHOOL, finishing out her final year, when the contest was announced. She was a solidly average student with, ahead of her, a solidly average set of expectations. She'd take a few business classes at the community college, probably; major in hospitality. Briefly—rebelliously—she'd considered becoming an aesthetician after picking up a brochure at the annual job fair hosted in the school gymnasium, but no one else she knew was going that route, and she had quickly put the idea out of her mind.

When considering a career as a hair and nails specialist is the only way you can think to beat the system, it's time to seriously reconsider your options. That's what Sabrina thought when she first heard about the contest.

It was a chance in a million. By the time Sabrina sent in her name—roughly fifteen minutes after the contest was announced—entries already numbered close to 25,000. It was almost comforting to watch the figure on the contest website continue to climb: 36,000 . . . 47,365 . . . 75,892 . . . 438,478 . . . 1,034,349 . . . The number, superimposed in white over an image of the red planet, flashed above the banner heading that ran across the centre of the screen:

THE LAST FRONTIER.

The printed reminder—in smaller font, at the bottom of the screen—that "anyone can become a pioneer" seemed logically supported by the continuously rolling numbers just above. All you had to do, the rules stipulated (after you clicked on the text block "anyone"), was enter your email address and, in 140 characters or less, your reason for leaving planet Earth.

Sabrina and her friend Amanda entered as a kind of a joke. "What do I need a hundred and forty characters for?" Sabrina had said. She'd typed out, "Why the hell not?," shoved her screen at Amanda, who laughed, then hit Send.

Two weeks later, she got a call from the TV station. She'd been randomly selected to attend the first elimination round. She'd nearly hung up. The pert voice on the line had opened with "Congratulations! You've won . . ." sounding just like one of those telemarketing calls she regularly hung up on. There was always some catch: even if they said that it was, nothing was ever actually free.

Later, Sabrina found herself going back to that moment. Over and over, in her mind, she received the call: "Congratulations! You've won . . ." And over and over—without knowing what bogus offer was going to come next: a contest she hadn't entered, a subscription she didn't want for a magazine she'd never read— she practised hanging up the phone.

That was key. She had to not know what was being offered— what was on the other end of the line. Because even now, even after everything that had happened, she knew that once she knew, once she heard the words "out of millions of applicants, you . . ." there was no going back. That even after the fact, in her mind, she would never be able to put down the phone.

———

It had been exhausting and humiliating. There was no other way to put it. The first elimination round had been a whirlwind of trivia and strength competitions, dance-offs, cook-offs, and empathy trials. But despite a gruelling seven hours deliberately designed to wear down both her physical and emotional endurance, Sabrina had endured. In part, this was because she still couldn't see the whole thing as anything more than a terrific joke. Sooner or later, she thought, it would all be over, and she would only laugh about it all. As she cleared away someone's dishes or checked them in or out of a hotel, she'd say: "I came this close to leaving all of this behind . . ."

In the evenings she would post a comment or two online, then for an hour or more continually press the refresh button on her screen and watch as the comments poured in. She'd barely read them—she just liked to see the number of responses steadily rise. It was amazing to think that all those people were out there. In any given moment. Watching and listening, cheering her on—toward what? It had been impossible to think past the bright lights of the set, the studio applause, the rush and confusion of being ushered on or off stage. It had been equally impossible to think of her followers (which now numbered several million) as anything more than mere numbers—filling seats, or ticking steadily away on the screen.

After making it to the fourth qualifying round, Sabrina and the rest of the eighteen remaining contestants were provided with a personal coach. Sabrina was assigned Dana Skools, a retired marketing analyst who meticulously debriefed each challenge with her and discussed strategies for the next. At the end of the day, though, it always came down to the same thing. Skools repeated it like a mantra. "Just keep doing what you're doing," she told Sabrina. "Be yourself." It was important, Skools explained, that Sabrina not "over-perform." If possible, in fact, she should aim to perform just an (almost imperceptible) notch *below* average. This was the sweet spot, counselled Skools. It accessed audience sympathy without tipping into disdain.

What was extraordinary about Sabrina was that, without really trying, she hit the sweet spot every time.

If, at the end of each successful round she felt a mounting dread, it was always inextricably tied with a dizzy delight. She had never before won anything in her life—not even a raffle or a door prize. She had never been the one called up onstage at a community function to accept a wrapped box of chocolates or a screen-printed hat. The few times she had participated in team sports at school she had, without ever really contributing to it, found herself on the losing end. So this was really the first time she felt what it meant to win. The surge, the rush . . . a sort of explosion in the brain. Once or twice, it occurred to her to regret that she'd never felt it before. Perhaps she would have pushed herself a little further, tried a little harder. But then again, she would think—with a distinct mixture of dread and delight—how much further could you get than Mars?

———

It lasted six months, but at the end of it, it was "without really knowing how it happened" that Sabrina Lowe-Mackey found herself preparing to leave the planet Earth.

There were seven of them in total who had made it to the final round—a contest that would take place, over an indefinite period of time, on the surface of the red planet. There was Hisham of the photographic memory; Lupe, the earth mother; Greg, the survivalist; Mary Ellen, the computer whiz; Brock, the nurse and all around "good guy"; Nadar, the diva. And then Sabrina, who was just . . . Sabrina. Really, there was nothing to distinguish her in any way. And though her ratings had never exactly soared like Greg's or Nadar's, they had remained consistently just above average, securing her an all-round third-place finish and a spot on a spaceship headed to THE LAST FRONTIER.

Of course she had reservations. Plenty of them. She was frightened half out of her wits, and was not ashamed to say so. Her candidness on the subject had in fact earned her major points in the final elimination rounds. When she met with her friends and her family in those last, weightless months before takeoff, she would tell them—admittedly, only half-convinced by her own words—that the fact that she was scared was precisely the reason she had to go. What if Galileo had hesitated before announcing that the Earth revolved around the Sun? If Vespucci had decided to stay home instead?

"For the first time in my life," Sabrina told her mother, father, and her old friend Amanda (now at the local college, completing the first semester of a hospitality program), "I have the opportunity to make a difference."

All this was televised of course—broadcast in real time into roughly a billion homes. For the seventy-two hours leading up to the actual moment of takeoff, there was constant coverage: interviews and "pioneer" profiles; features on space food, technology, and entertainment; mental and physical training sessions; team-building initiatives. Even when Sabrina and the six other pioneers went home for a final meal with their families, the camera teams hovered above them like hungry, uninvited guests.

It was amazing how quickly they got used to it. When Sabrina had watched reality shows in the past, she'd always imagined that everyone was actually talking to the camera—even if they weren't supposed to be, or thought they weren't. But it was easier than she'd thought to just be herself—as Dana Skools had instructed. And she could nearly always count on becoming (thanks to a brilliant team of editors who—except when the show was in real time—expertly cut and compressed everything into fifty-minute blocks) more "herself" at the end of the day than she had been at any point during it.

Later, when all she had was time on her hands, she spent a lot of it rewatching all sixty-seven episodes that had been aired before takeoff—and then a lot of the unedited material as well. It was funny, but it was always the hours of uncut footage that felt surreal and strange to her when she watched them later, and the carefully edited episodes that felt somehow "right." It really was incredible, she reflected, the way the editors had managed to distill everything in such a way that the episodes ended up feeling more true to life than real life ever did.

It was all a matter of perspective, of course, and the trick—
Sabrina considered—to life, as well as to television, was in
finding a way of seeing things from the outside—and yourself
as just another part of a larger story. A story that, though you
might not know where it's headed, or what part in it you will
ultimately play, has a genuine arc and is progressing toward
some inevitable end.

Based on the immense popularity of the show's first season, the
producers bragged that it wouldn't be long before successive
seasons of The Last Frontier sent enough pioneers to populate
the entire planet. But almost before the first pioneers left the
Earth's atmosphere, the show's ratings began to drop. Six months
later—the moment everyone had been waiting for—when the
pioneers first set foot on Mars, real-time coverage dwindled to
an hour-long nightly recap. Six months after that, the program
was cut to a once-a-week half-hour segment—which, when commercial time was taken into consideration, really only amounted
to something less than twenty minutes.

Nobody talked anymore about future seasons—and nobody
talked about bringing the pioneers home.

Of course, once it became clear the way things were going,
everyone said they "could have seen it coming." Everything—
even, or rather especially, reality—has a shelf life, after all, and
really (the producers all said) there had never been any reason not
to expect a gradual loss of interest. They weren't in much of a position to complain: by the time the show entered its "final round,"
they'd made their money back on the launch six times over.

For a while, there were the usual attempts to keep the energy, and the ratings, up. A few relatively tedious romantic dramas developed naturally or were invented. A baby was conceived, then born. (Ten months after blast-off, Nadar gave birth to a baby girl: Adara, named for the brightest star in the sky.) More valuable than those who celebrated the birth were those who condemned it. It was one thing to banish seven consenting adults to another planet, dissenters opined, but quite another to banish an unborn child. For a few weeks after the news broke that Nadar was expecting, and then again after the baby was born, protests were staged in Washington, Paris, Toronto, Beijing. "Save our star!" "Bring Adara home!"

Ratings on both occasions soared—but there was no way, the show's writers complained, to build on the story without actually bringing the kid home (something the station had made clear from the beginning was frankly impossible).

They were being cut off, Sabrina understood, finally. The realization had been slow at first, but she couldn't fool herself forever: it had been a long time since she'd felt that "real time" was progressing toward anything—well, real. No, it wouldn't be long at all, she lamented candidly into the camera one night, until the red planet's first pioneers were left to themselves, the camera gaping at them uselessly above. Until there was no one left to cut or edit or rearrange, let alone to actually witness the material of their lives.

THE ACCOUNT

LET US BEGIN IN THE USUAL WAY, AT THE BEGINNING.

Although even on this point, our party was frankly divided. Our stated ambition—five hundred years to the day after the shipwreck of Álvar Núñez Cabeza de Vaca at what is now the port of Galveston—was to retrace the uncertain route that explorer took across a continent that was still yet to be "discovered." And yet how, exactly, we were going to do so was by no means clear.[1]

It was absolutely necessary, some—rather vocal—members of our party maintained, that any re-enactment of de Vaca's journey begin from Spain. And yet, it was rejoined, even if we began by retracing de Vaca's route from the Old World to the New (adding, as might be imagined, untold financial and logistical complications to what had been, until this point, a relatively modest proposal), it would still be necessary to establish some point of departure. Would it not, then, be just as well to begin from the much more readily accessible Galveston shore?

Perhaps it would be more fitting (one member suggested) to begin neither "here" nor "there" but at the summit of the long-extinct volcano on the largest of the Canary Islands, the last

---

1   It is well known that the account of de Vaca's journey is riddled with numerous errors in both chronology and geography. We therefore pledged that our own retracing of it would be, of necessity, both erratic and undisciplined.

lava of which had not flowed in roughly one thousand years. We
might follow the same route de Vaca once did—after his appointment as governor of those recently conquered isles. Might, from
that vantage point, stare off—as he once, doubtless, did—toward
where, at the farthest limit of vision, the ocean gave way, not to
emptiness, but to other limits, other unknown shores.

But if (it was countered) we were going to cast back that far
in both distance and time, we might just as well cast even further. Begin in the little Andalusian town, midway between the
mountains and the sea, where de Vaca was born. Or at the mountain pass—once, apparently, marked by the head of a cow—
through which the King of Navarre was once led to safety by an
illustrious ancestor of little Álvar.[2]

But the costs of beginning at such a remote crossroads in
both space and time, and not any other perhaps equally valid,
and doubtless more accessible, location, led us to put these ideas
quite out of our mind. (And was that not, we reasoned amongst
ourselves, the *very meaning* of history: to arrive at—and embark
from—if not exactly the beginning, a *place* to begin?)

And so we began our expedition, as had been initially proposed, on Galveston Island, in front of the Seaview vacation
condos, adjacent to the pier.

We fashioned rafts of approximately the same shape and size
as those the explorer had constructed for himself and his men,
and stumbled from them onto the "unknown" shore.

---

2   An event that led, more or less directly, to the eventual conquest of
    the Muslim Moors, and earned the illustrious ancestor (along with
    generations to follow) the name of the animal's body part that had
    pointed the way.

We looked about. Wondered, like de Vaca, if (though we had been blown terribly off course and lost over half of our men) we had not, after all, reached our intended destination.[3]

Without being certain, we set out across the highway, past Reef Realty and Supply and Demand Wholesale Lumber, then plunged bravely into the empty lot behind Gulf Coast Plaza where, almost immediately, we got hung up in a large swamp. After a lengthy and sometimes heated discussion, we decided to bypass the wettest regions by following the Aughsten Road. We had agreed to avoid any pre-existing highways, but this decision had been contentious from the outset. It was argued that the explorer himself would have been only too eager to follow any road or pathway that presented itself to him. To specifically avoid any route that had already been travelled was—these more opportunist members of our group maintained—to be unfaithful to the spirit and the intention of the original voyage.

And yet, as others rejoined, more pertinent to our overall intention was the reclamation of some sense—and by whatever means possible—of the unexpected.

It was necessary to remind ourselves of this again when, just after noon, we found ourselves arrested by the local police for trespassing on the grounds of a private home. This misadventure delayed us by nearly a week, and when we were finally able to clear ourselves of charges (with the help

---

3 Arriving on the Galveston coast, Álvar Núñez Cabeza de Vaca wondered if he had, in fact, reached La Florida, as had been his intention. After all, it is difficult to know, when arriving in a place you have never been, if it is or is not the place you have been looking for.

of a local lawyer, who also happened to be a history enthusi-
ast and an amateur thespian) and continue on our way, we
found ourselves beset by a swarm of reporters and several
camera crews.

Though we tried our best to behave naturally in front of the
cameras, we were always, at least in some sense, aware that our
every movement was being recorded—that whatever we did or
said might potentially be broadcast live across the country or, by
some accounts, the world.

One positive outcome of all of this was that we were no
longer troubled by a particularly contentious issue we had not
yet resolved: the problem of how we were going to recreate
the purported enslavement of Cabeza de Vaca and fifteen of
his men. It was now believed that references to slavery in de
Vaca's account were intended only metaphorically; that, far
from enslaving the European adventurers, the Native inhabitants of the Gulf Coast region acted instead as guardians and
saviours to the unfortunate crew. It is in any case quite clear
that without a Native presence on the island, Cabeza de Vaca
would certainly have perished along with the rest of his men—
and with them, every trace of their voyage.

We agreed on the following point: that the media attention—which we'd at first unanimously bemoaned as distracting
and inauthentic—proved as apt an analogy as we were likely to
hit upon for the sort of scrutiny Cabeza de Vaca and his fifteen
men would have experienced upon first drifting onto Texan
shores. They, too, we reflected, would at the very least have
felt—as we did—"not quite themselves" in being examined so
closely, and through such a distinctly foreign lens. They, too,

would have felt vulnerable to disapproval, censure, and every other imaginable attack.

And yet, it was not all bad. Our story had reached every corner of the country—had even wrapped around the globe! Everywhere we went the local inhabitants clamoured to greet us. Buses arrived and dumped out tourists who snapped photographs. People opened their homes, delivered us blankets and food. For the most part, the weather held, and—because of our following—food was always plentiful. It would have been easy to grow complacent, even lazy. But for the sake of authenticity, we sometimes foraged for food among the restaurant and fish shack dumpsters, or even purposely went hungry—fasting, sometimes for several days.

Though the frank admiration and festive mood that greeted us was a stark contrast to the reticence and suspicion that had met de Vaca and his crew, we often reminded ourselves that our reception was not unlike the reception of the great explorer during the latter years of his wanderings. Throngs of people gathered to greet him, to reach out toward him as he passed— everybody desperately hoping they might find themselves touched, even healed, through simple proximity to something that they didn't understand.

And so it goes. We were propelled, just as history is propelled, by our own story, which preceded us, and by which (in the form of both the television crews and this account, which had not yet been written) we were followed. We witnessed it, our own journey, in the eyes of the people who lined the streets of the towns we passed through, the highways we crossed, the rivers we forded, and the parking lots in which we slept and foraged for food. Recognized in their frank expressions, and the way they lifted their arms to hail us as we went, the same simple expectation that had prompted us to begin our own voyage—to strike off, into whatever wilderness remains. An expectation that the world, despite the ways in which it has so far been described, can bend and change; that the blank spaces on the map can be filled in, made known.

And when at night we lay huddled together under the bleachers of an abandoned stadium, or the awning of a bus stop, or under the simple, open air, we often spoke of what we might offer these people. What message might we trail—as de Vaca once did—like a scent through the wilderness? What words, what message might we, five hundred years later, and in good faith, pass on? What could we say? How could we willingly progress, while still remaining loyal to the operations both of history and of the human heart—each of which beats only because it doesn't know how or why it first began beating, or if or when it will stop?

THE LESSON

MY FATHER HAD BEEN PART OF THE FAMOUS LOST BATTALION, one of forty-six men of the 307th and 308th Infantry who walked out of the Argonne Forest after everyone else had been killed, wounded, taken prisoner, or had otherwise disappeared.

He found God in those woods, he would say. Standing in full dress uniform at the front of the revival tent, on the makeshift stage my brother and I had hammered together mere hours before, he would shout, "I was lost! But now, now I've been found!" He would work himself into such a fury as he spoke that it was difficult to tell, sometimes, where he left off speaking of the Meuse-Argonne offensive and began speaking of the fire and brimstone that awaited the unlucky in hell.

My brother and I would run through the crowd holding our empty hats in our hands.

"And did we surrender?" my father would ask, shaking his fist at the air. "We could not help but doubt, but did we—even once—think of surrendering to the enemy, though they had us surrounded on every side?"

Our hats grew heavier, then heavier still. So I came to understand something, and from a young age: that there is a cost to everything, even the opening and closing of the human heart. It is an invisible cost, but it is a cost nonetheless, and this knowledge, gleaned from the words of my father as they became physical objects, which I collected from the crowd—my first lesson in the simple economics of the human soul—stands me in good stead even now, long after I have ceased to believe in the words, in God, or in my father.

For as long as I could remember, it had been my father's custom to escort one or two of his most devout followers—of the female persuasion—to our tent at night. With these young devotees we shared our evening meal, and my father would relate a story or two from the time he had spent in the Argonne Forest.

"We were not lost in the ordinary sense of the word. Oh no! We knew exactly where we were the whole time. And so did command headquarters, and so, too, did the Germans. It was because of this, after all—because everyone in the world knew exactly where we were, including the enemy—that we were lost. As in"—here my father would pause and, without any trouble, seek out the eyes of the faithful—"desperate," my father would say. "As in, beyond hope." After dropping his gaze, he would continue brusquely. "Our mission, however," he'd say, "was to hold our position at any cost. Even though we knew we had been cut off—that we were now surrounded by the enemy on every side. Even though we could hear the voices of German officers as they called out roll in the morning!

"All day long we were barraged by enemy fire. Men dropped silently. Screams were swallowed, or stuffed into mouths like rags. There was no mess call, as we had eaten all our food, and it was bitter cold without our winter garments, which—in order to aid our travel—we had purposely left behind. We had only our weapons and two pigeons—the second-to-last of which was released before noon.

"Our message was simple: 'Cannot support be sent at once?'

"Almost at once, and very simply, an answer came. We recognized our own artillery fire peppering the hills to the south, and rejoiced. But then a round landed in our own pocket. Then another, and another. There was nothing for us to do but dive into our holes and lie still, like dead men. Above us, the earth shook with the rattle and roar of our own guns. Our holes collapsed, burying some of us alive. Those of us who emerged did so to find that the heavy shelling had stripped away the dense brush and trees that had served as our only protection.

"It was into this devastated landscape, toward a horizon empty of all but the barest of forms, that our last pigeon, the veteran carrier, Cher Ami, was sent with our final message. A message that—attesting again to the fact that we were not and had never been lost in any physical sense—described our exact position along the 276th parallel, and concluded: 'For heaven's sake, stop it.'

"We watched. All of us together, the living and the dead. Our faces turned toward the open sky as our only hope—our Cher Ami—flitted first this way, then that, dodging enemy bullets as she went. She seemed to hover, rather than fly, as if suspended by our own desire. When she rested, taking what shelter she could in the lower branches of a blasted tree, we urged her on from below with words—then with a few well-placed stones. When she took off once more, flying directly into the enemy fire"—here again my father sought the faithful's eye—"we saw the impact," he said. "Saw her stutter, fall—recover slightly—then, wavering, continue on, out of sight, finally disappearing from our view, like water evaporating slowly in air."

It was always some comfort to me, after this particular story, to hear the commotion my father made as my brother and I waited outside. I knew, you see, that if I heard my father's grunts and the cries of the faithful, who, even after my father had sworn in agony and was quiet, would continue to softly call out, that my father would soon be in a generous mood. But it was precisely into this comforting quiet, when just the pleasant, lingering sobs of the faithful could be heard, that the trouble burst one night. A light flared and a low murmur of voices grew to a muffled roar. Without a word, my brother and I crept together into my father's tent in order to warn him—just as a gun, firing in the near distance, did our work for us.

At the sound of the gun, the faithful—who just a moment before had been sleeping, blissfully unaware, at my father's side—shrieked, and at that exact moment she saw us. Our eyes glittering, no doubt, like the eyes of animals in the dim light. I saw her naked breasts swing, and I recall thinking how unbearably heavy they appeared as she stumbled in the near dark, reaching blindly for her clothes.

My father's pale backside was visible to us, too. He lumbered up like a drunken bear, then stood gazing at us—our faces by now, and not merely our eyes, apparent to him as the light from the approaching torches flared briefly in our direction. Not half-lit, half-fallen in shadow, but flickering; visible only half of the

time. Now you could see us, now you could not. This was also
the way that our father appeared to us. One moment he was illuminated—larger than life—and the next he had disappeared
from view. But as the crowd approached there was less and less
time in which our father did not appear to us, and finally there
was no time at all. We stood together, illuminated by an unbearable blinding light.

I had always known the way the story ended: my father, gazing
up at the sky as Cher Ami made her final flight; the buzzer sounding in the pigeon loft at division headquarters; a Signal Corps
officer peering in to see which of the little birds had arrived; his
finding there none other than little Cher Ami . . . Imagine! It was
nothing less than a miracle! Shot in the chest, blinded in one eye,
and covered in blood, she still carried her message.

I had, countless times, heard my father conclude the story in
the following way: "And so at last our voices were heard, and we
were delivered"; had heard him proclaim, therefore, the proximity between ourselves and God (whose judgment, he vowed,
would soon be upon us). I had as many times heard him promise
salvation to all those possessed of the courage and strength, like
the forty-six men of the 307th and 308th Infantry, NOT TO
SURRENDER. And yet I had not, until that moment, realized . . .
I did believe. I, too, was one of my father's faithful.

But it wasn't only belief that I felt then. It was more than
that.

I saw it. I felt it. The combined judgment of heaven and hell
as it entered me, and just in that exact moment, I heard a voice

outside and it spoke, saying, "We know you are in there, you son of a bitch." And then the light by which we were illuminated burst in upon us, rending a gaping hole in the side of the tent. We smelled the canvas as it began to burn.

From behind, my father gave both my brother and me a shove.

"Run!" he shouted.

Hand in hand, we ran. We could hear the steady rhythm of our father's breath as he followed, and I didn't know if I was running away from him or from the light, or from God himself. When finally we stopped, however, neither my father nor God were anywhere to be found, and I realized that the heavy, winded breathing that had chased me down the hill had been my own.

All night we crouched, my brother and I, in the cold grass, which, as darkness gradually faded with the first light of day, became wet with dew. The dew gathered on our eyelids, on our bare elbows, on the ends of our noses, and we shivered and shook as though, indeed, the final judgment had come.

But in fact it was only the dampness of another early morning, rising almost exactly like the last.

MR. DOYLE'S
ANCESTRAL
GENETIC
HOMELAND

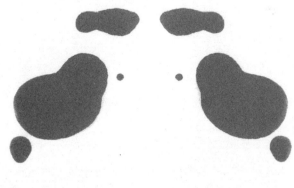

MAVIE DOYLE HAD LIVED IN GRAND ISLAND, NEBRASKA, her whole life, until, in January of 2003, her son, Fred, who had made his name in real estate in the late nineties, left New York and bought a sprawling house in a quiet suburb just outside Old Saybrook, Connecticut. It was at this time that Fred Doyle invited his mother to live with him in a small, self-contained unit located on the western edge of the property.

To say "invited" is not perhaps quite accurate, however. As with everything Fred did, there had been no room for negotiation. He had simply announced the move to his mother over the phone one Sunday afternoon during one of their weekly chats—which Fred, bless his heart, had never neglected. Not even during the heady days of his initial success with Doyle and Sons—the company he'd managed to get off the ground back in 1994, on little more than (as Mavie always put it, proudly) a wing and a prayer.

Fred had been only recently out of law school then, and everyone else was still reeling from the hard blow of the recession. He'd been a late bloomer; had frittered away most of his twenties and was now almost entirely unable to account for them. But, still, he'd managed to land a spot at St. John's Law School, and was able to pay for it himself, with the last of the fairly sizeable sum he'd inherited from his father. Usher Doyle, an oilman, had left Texas sometime in the early fifties for Nebraska—though no one, including Mavie, had known why. It had been almost "certifi-able," Mavie had said at the time. Now she said, smugly: "Foresight surely ran in the family." Though he never lived to see it, it made both Mavie and Fred sentimental to see how the money was now flowing into the state—just as quickly and as plentifully as the oil flowed out.

Four years at law school had taught Fred to declare that there was no future in law—that it would be wiser to get into real estate. He sold off what was left of his father's claim, and didn't lose too much sleep over it. By the time Mavie came to live with him in Connecticut, there was nothing left but the old Grand Island house—a modest enough two-storey on a residential street that eventually sold well below market value. (But that was just fine, Fred told her, because everything else—including the scattered holdings up in western Nebraska that Usher had bought the year Fred was born, on spec—had sold at a signifi-cant profit.)

The important thing, after all—as Fred always said—was not knowing when to get in, but when to get out. In 2003, every-thing was telling him to get out. It was the Towers, for one thing, he said, his big head waving a little from side to side as he spoke and looking like (if he were physically capable of doing so) he might even cry. Fred had never cried in his life; he was pretty sure it was genetic—a tear duct issue. His father had once mentioned something to that effect. You see, it was from his father, Usher Doyle, that Fred had "inherited" his interest in the subject of genetics. It was a natural inclination; a way of addressing (Usher, and then Fred, always said) some of life's most basic, and most pressing, questions. A way of feeling (and here Fred's voice, as he repeated his father's words, would catch slightly in his throat, though he still wouldn't, or couldn't, cry) the way that, though it didn't often seem it, everything was *connected* somehow.

Fred was childless. By the time he and his wife, Bea—whom he'd met in his first year of law school and married a year after that—pulled up and moved from New York to Connecticut, they had been trying for nine years. When Fred graduated and immediately launched Doyle and Sons, the name had been an optimistic gesture. Later on, however, he emphasized its success as a marketing ploy. "People like" (he'd told his wife, and anyone else who asked) "*continuity*. If I just say to you, Fred Doyle, what do you care? You want to know, who is this Doyle? What happens when he's gone?"

Bea had been twenty-seven when they married. Nine years later, she was thirty-six and beginning to lose hope. "You are two healthy individuals," one doctor after another had told them. "These things sometimes just take a little time." Fred had done his best to console his wife, but as the years passed it became increasingly difficult, and he could not get it out of his head that she blamed him a little—even though she was careful to say that she didn't.

Fred was certain it would do Bea good to get out of the city. "The fresh air," he said. "All that space . . ."

But Bea did not want to move. She was happy in the city, she told Fred. Though she knew that this was technically incorrect. In truth, she was simply afraid that she would be *more* unhappy in the country, with nothing but Fred and Mavie and a bunch of fresh air.

But officially, if anyone asked, Fred always said they had moved out of town because of the Towers. They just made me rethink everything, he said. From a real estate perspective, if nothing else. "I had to ask myself," he'd say, "where is the future?" in a way that made whomever he was speaking to feel, for some reason they probably couldn't even identify, suddenly very sorry for Fred Doyle.

There was just something about him. Even at the zenith of his real estate career, when things could not have been going any better, you couldn't help feeling a sort of pity for him. The sort of pity you might feel for a caged gorilla. Because despite—or because of—anything he said out loud, you knew he was always acting on pure animal instinct. That it was all about self-protection—and fear. You could almost see his hackles raised, for example, as he went about quietly selling Doyle and Sons and making arrangements for the purchase of the Old Saybrook house.

But even with all of his obligations in the city, he had managed a trip out to Nebraska, to help his mother pack. The house had become something of a museum over the years, in homage to Mavie's personal family history. The walls were plastered with ancestral photos, all of which had been blown up at least several times their original size so that they appeared pointillist, nearly abstract. The faces of the relatives on both sides of the family had been so blanched of detail that it was nearly impossible to tell them apart.

That's where the stories came in. Mavie talked endlessly, given even the slightest opportunity. About her parents: John MacArthur, a Scot who had landed in Boston but almost immediately made his way west. And a certain Josephine Aiken, by some reports a mute. It was only (Mavie later said) that she didn't speak to strangers. In fact, some of Mavie's earliest memories were of her mother singing. Less a memory than a physical trait. She could still feel those songs, Mavie said. Inside her. Ancient Omaha songs; nearly tuneless, and in a language she couldn't understand. "But that voice!" she would say, closing her eyes as though she were hearing it still.

It was always convincing. Watching Mavie remembering the songs her mother sang to her as a child would almost make you think you remembered them, too. In fact, Mavie had had some success in her youth as an amateur actor. Even through the hard years after Fred's birth—through a series of miscarriages and subsequent "nervous complaints." She would often become disoriented, actually begin to behave differently, dress in other people's clothes. She would put on the ancient headdress that had somehow come into her possession, and slip into something of a trance.

The headdress had been passed down to her from her grandfather, Mavie said—an Omaha chief. The fact that the headdress was not actually Omaha did not trouble Mavie particularly. It was a fact that had first been pointed out by Fred, at the age of only ten, after returning from a class trip to the local museum. When Fred told his mother that the headdress was not Omaha in style, and even looked it up in a book in order to prove it to her, Mavie had merely shrugged. She was proud of him for having an inquiring mind, but there was an awful lot—she said—you couldn't learn in a book.

Especially after Usher died, Mavie's ancestors developed even more of a presence around the house. Where once, for example, the story of Grandma Josephine's Omaha lineage had been vague enough for Usher to have pronounced it, once, little more than a euphemism for her having always been "a little strange," over the years it became increasingly concrete. The "museum pieces"—at one time mere decorative objects, which had helped to create in the house a certain whimsical mood—likewise developed concrete, if shifting, historical explanations and roots. Aside from the headdress, the most impressive item by far was a nearly life-sized cigar store Indian, which for some reason that no one remembered had been nicknamed Major Stokes.

Mavie Doyle had been pretty heavily medicated since the early 1980s, and still dutifully took her prescribed dose of lithium every morning with her breakfast cereal, so—though she hadn't actually *become* her ancestors in a long, long time, and her medical treatment kept her just this side of genuinely daft—she liked to be surrounded by her "people."

By the time Fred arrived to help his mother pack, it was difficult to move in the house without bumping into a museum relic. This seemed fairly deliberate on Mavie's part, because every time Fred did so—as he edged his way around an end table piled with turquoise jewellery, for example, or brushed against a wall hung with tapestries and beadwork and the two or three genuine Remington sketches she had somehow managed to acquire—Mavie would launch into each object's long history.

On the couple of occasions Bea visited, she and Fred would catch one another's eye as Mavie spoke. It was a rare pleasure for the two of them to exchange a look like this. To demonstrate with a raised eyebrow or a shrug that they were in agreement on at least this one thing: they didn't believe—and had never believed—a word that Mavie said.

When Fred visited with Bea, he never interrupted his mother when she spoke. The two of them would listen patiently—eyebrows raised—as Mavie told them, for example, the story of her great-grandmother, a Navajo princess who had been kidnapped three times: once by the Mexicans, and twice by the Americans. Each time, her great-grandmother—Navajo princess and warrior—had escaped. She had trekked hundreds of miles, and slept in trees; she had fended off jaguars; collected rainwater in the seams of leaves; had even, briefly, been adopted by a pack of wolves.

It was not as difficult as Fred had initially thought it might be to persuade his mother to move. The biggest hurdle was convincing her that not all of the museum "artifacts" could be moved into the Old Saybrook unit—that the bulk of the collection would have to be placed in storage. Then deciding which ones. Of course, getting rid of anything was absolutely out of the question, and Fred knew enough not to even bring it up. The items were—as they had always been—"for the grandchildren." Mavie was apparently untroubled by the long period of time that Bea and Fred had so far remained childless and continued to speak of the grandchildren without batting an eye.

When Fred explained to Bea why they'd be paying a monthly storage fee on top of the cost of moving Mavie to Connecticut and caring for her in their home, Bea wondered seriously if Fred had also gone mad. She had been on her way out of their nearly empty Park Avenue kitchen, but now she stopped—turned. From Fred's perspective, with the light coming in from the curtainless window, setting her thin figure in stark relief, she appeared almost two-dimensional.

"Fred," she said slowly, "we don't have any children." Then, just in case he really didn't understand: "There won't"—her voice faltered, but remained firm, almost cruel—"*be* any grandchildren, *Fred*."

Instinct, Mavie called it. Like his father before him, Fred had always had "good instinct." For example, when he pulled out of real estate and moved his family to the quiet community of Old Saybrook, Connecticut, the market was less than two years away from completely bottoming out. Even the country's top economists had failed to see it coming, and it would become a great mystery afterward how no one but Fred Doyle had bothered to contemplate the internal limit to economic growth, until it was far too late.

When the crash did come, and everyone else was trying desperately to get out from under, Fred had already been living in Old Saybrook for going on five years, and Mavie—well settled in her adjacent apartment—was talking proudly of how her entire legacy would very soon be passed on to Rebecca Doyle, the adopted Chinese daughter of Fred and Bea.

Rebecca had been twenty-two months old when Bea and Fred brought her home; now, at nearly four, she delighted in her grandmother's collection. She was especially fond of placing the headdress (once worn by her great-great-grandfather, an Omaha chief) on her head and peering out from under it with a four-year-old's self-conscious grin. "That will go directly to you one day," Mavie would say, taking evident pleasure in the fact that the headdress would bypass Fred (and, in this way, making it for the first time absolutely clear that Fred's comment, at the age of ten, which Mavie had brushed off blithely and never mentioned again, had in fact deeply wounded her).

For all of them, then, Rebecca signified a new beginning. But it would be wrong to assume, based on this, that things had become easy between Fred and Bea. In fact, tensions in the household rose to an all-time high immediately after Rebecca's arrival, then remained that way. To make matters worse, it was becoming increasingly apparent that the line between fantasy and reality, if it ever existed for Mavie, had disappeared entirely. This was not the first time this had happened, of course, but at her age, Fred reflected, it would no doubt be the last.

All of Mavie's earlier "breaks" had occurred while Fred had still been in grade school, and it was entirely possible—as Bea pointed out more than once—that every strategy Fred had so far developed in life had been in reaction to that difficult period when his mother had made a fairly regular habit of losing her mind. Even his inability to cry, for example, may have been, she suggested, rather than a genetic trait handed down from his father, merely an adaptive response.

Fred was forced to consider the idea again one day when, in the middle of an especially tough therapy session with Bea, he touched his face and found it suddenly wet. He was so surprised that he almost laughed—but the laugh was so mixed up with whatever else he was feeling that it came out less like a laugh and more like an ugly sob.

So his tear ducts worked! He felt an immense sense of relief—then a strong desire to share that relief, and whatever else was occurring inside him (perhaps somewhere deep in his cellular structure), with his wife. But when, still sobbing, he looked up at Bea, he saw that she was looking back at him with a look of such pure disgust that it sent actual shivers up and down his spine, and made him cry harder—now from a deep sense of shame that he didn't understand.

They drove home silently—Bea in the passenger seat. She had her head turned slightly, so Fred couldn't catch her eye. It was a sunny June day, but the tinted window she gazed out of made everything look slightly grey.

Fred thought of Rebecca. Sitting in Major Stokes's lap at home, listening to Grandma Mavie's impossible stories—completely unsuspecting of the unspoken violence that had found its way into her parents' lives. A violence that—Fred understood in that moment—had already begun to quietly eat them up from the inside.

They wouldn't leave one another, Fred thought quickly—no. Neither one of them would ever have the courage. They would instead let whatever had begun to eat away at them continue to do so until one day, many years later, they would wake to discover that nothing held their lives together at all.

The thought troubled him. Again, he thought of Rebecca. She'd be hurt, of course; realize that her entire life to date had been a lie, and she would blame them for it. As well as for whatever complex constellation of personal issues she was confronted with then. Whatever those issues were, or were going to be, it was absolutely clear to Fred that every single one of them would eventually be traced back either to the bloodless war he was currently waging with his wife, or to his mother's madness. Rebecca was now blissfully unaware of both. How was she to know yet—or to care—where one story ended and the other began? Or what was true and what was false, and why it mattered?

Fred knew all of this and he also knew that there was nothing, in the face of it, any one of them would—or could—do. Because amidst it all, she was there. Rebecca. Perfect, and unsuspecting. The one true thing among all those lies.

Rebecca had just always *made sense* to Fred in a way that nothing else in his life ever had, and not only that, she made other things *make sense*, too—simply because she existed. So that if he ever regretted anything, or thought about changing his life, he was always brought up short because everything that had happened to him so far—all of the good things, as well as, or especially, the bad—had in some way, more or less directly, led to Rebecca. There was no way, therefore, to pick at the knot. No way of even *wanting* to pick at it, or to unravel anything.

And yet despite this—despite "instinct," intention, and every desire—things continued to unravel. Afterward, it would have been as impossible to isolate the exact moment in which things finally came undone as it would have been to deter-mine the exact combination of circumstances that led to the fortuitous arrival of Rebecca into their lives, but years later Bea would insist that such a moment had existed. It was the moment Fred sent away for the DNA testing kit he'd seen advertised online.

Bea had always been quietly tolerant of Fred's interest in genetics—an interest (as he often joked) he'd inherited from his father. But after Rebecca arrived, and though it was another thing that was always left unspoken between them, she couldn't help but see Fred's continued attention to the subject as a personal affront.

"You realize it's a bunch of Mormons," she said when Fred showed her the advertisement. "You'd be giving your DNA away to a bunch of Mormons, you know that."

Fred shrugged. "I'd consider it a bonus," he said, "if, on top of everything else, there's even a slight chance of a retroactive conversion." He grinned at her. "Who knows? You might be looking at the future proprietor of an entire small planet!"

Bea had been about to put the dinner on and was holding a can of organic chickpeas in one hand and a can opener in the other. Very deliberately, she put the chickpeas down on the counter, then turned toward Fred. She held the can opener between them like a knife.

"How dare you," she hissed.

Fred's grin vanished. He looked perplexed—but said nothing. They could hear strains of Rebecca's favourite TV show drifting in from the next room.

"How. Dare. You," Bea said again, louder. Then she dropped the can opener and left the room. Shortly after, she apologized. She had no idea, she said, what had come over her. And it was not until much later—long after she and Rebecca had moved back to the city, Mavie had been transferred to an assisted living home, and Fred had fatally shot himself through the mouth—that she realized what had made her so unspeakably angry in that moment. She had understood something. For the first time—as Fred shrugged at her and grinned—she had realized it was not a joke, but instead perfectly true: Fred, if given the least opportunity, would leave behind not only her and Rebecca but the entire human race, for the mere whiff of a chance at his own far planet.

Meanwhile, Fred ordered Thai food to replace the dinner that never got made and sent a vial of his saliva away in the mail. Six weeks after that, he received a pie graph indicating that his genetic makeup was 99.9% Western European with the remaining .1% coming from somewhere in the Middle East. He must have stared for a full minute at the big blue circle in the centre of the page with its single sliver of orange before he could make any sense of what he saw.

The name Doyle, as Fred already knew well, came from the pre-tenth-century Gaelic Dhubhghall, or "dark stranger." The just barely visible sliver of orange on his chart was, at the very least, confirmation that a certain dark stranger had at some point prior to the tenth century wandered west.

Fred continued to stand there, looking at the pie graph and flipping through the five accompanying pages he'd been sent without entirely admitting to himself what he was looking for—or why he was surprised. Had he not spent his entire life—at least since the age of ten or eleven—doubting the origin and authenticity of his grandfather's "feather hat"? Had he not informed everyone—shamelessly, in front of his mother—that she was prone, at the very least, to "exaggeration"?

And yet, somehow, all this time (he realized it only now, as he leafed once more through six pages of printed material, no part of which offered him anything more than what he'd already glimpsed on the first page), he'd *believed*. If not exactly in the stories his mother told, then in the fact that they were *based* on something and so still were—in some fundamental, if unverifiable, and finally nearly irrelevant way—"true."

But—no. There was not a shred of truth to his mother's stories, he realized now. He was the genetic by-product of a slew of Western Europeans and a single dark stranger. He tried to feel okay about that. He folded the printout and slipped it back into its envelope, then walked the length of the yard to Mavie's unit at the back of the house. He raised his hand at the door—hesitated a moment. Knocked. The door was not closed, and in another moment, without waiting for a reply, he pushed it open and stepped inside. Mavie was sitting in her chair by the window, talking to the birds. They flocked to the yard because she regularly spilled birdseed and the remains of her own meals for them to peck at out there. Directly ahead of him sat Major Stokes, his wooden face stoic and inexpressive, betraying nothing.

"Mom," Fred said, staring hard at the Indian.

Mavie looked up.

Mavie was always delighted to see Fred, and this occasion was no different. "Fred!" she said as he entered—but then she saw the look on his face. "What is it, Fred?" she said. "Is anything wrong?"

Fred was still staring hard at Major Stokes but his mother's voice interrupted him and—strangely embarrassed for some reason—he dropped his gaze.

"No," he told his mother. "No, nothing." He sat down stiffly in a chair across from Mavie, but felt distracted, annoyed. He wondered what Bea and Rebecca were doing back at the house; the thought of them caused him to half-start from his chair.

"Fred," Mavie said. "Are you sure you're all right?"

"Of course," Fred said. But a few minutes later he excused himself and headed hurriedly across the short lawn.

He plunged into the house as though it were on fire. "Bea?" he called. "Rebecca?" There was no answer and, since it was Wednesday and the cleaning lady had just come, there was no indication that the house was lived in at all.

"Bea!" Fred called again. "Bea! Rebecca!" He headed toward the stairs and took them two at a time.

At the landing, he paused. His face was hot by now, and streaming with tears—but he didn't feel sad. He felt only the terrific force of his blood as it beat in his throat, the panic of sudden joy in his chest as Rebecca's voice rang out in reply.

THE NOVELIST

AT EIGHT O'CLOCK, when Gil sat down to his desk with his first cup of coffee, the kids would still be out in the hall—pulling on their shoes and wrestling into their coats. Alice would be yelling reminders to them from the kitchen: not to forget their lunches, or be late, or stop anywhere on the way home. Then the kids and Alice would hustle out the door and the door would shut firmly. Gil would be left alone—plunged suddenly into near-perfect silence.

He had recently sent away for a computer program that allowed him to diagram his thought process onscreen, and he now had an elaborate map linking various prompts (FLASHBACK SEQUENCE, MISE EN ABYME), a series of quotations culled from a set of inspirational texts he kept within easy reach on his desk (Plato's *Sophist*, H. Charlton Bastian's *Evolution and Origin of Life*), and every half-thought or petty observation he imagined might become somehow relevant once things began to fall into place.

It was a decent enough system, he told Alice over dinner one night, except that it was limited to two dimensions. His best thoughts never occurred to him singly, after all, but seemed to take place one on top of the other, as if all at once. When he was forced to isolate them, he explained—write them down—they always appeared as if they existed discretely, suggesting an order and a logical causality he could in no way attribute to the actual functioning of his own mind. In addition (Gil complained to Alice), he'd managed to fill up an entire screen in a single week and would now be obliged to scroll either up or down in order to see how his thoughts either connected to one another or failed to. Only a week in, he lamented, and he was right back to where he'd started, because observing certain, select connections in his thought process was pretty much what he'd always been capable of—with or without a computer program.

At 10:45—after spending precisely two and half hours staring at, and attempting to retrace, his thoughts on the screen—he would get up and make himself a cheese sandwich. He would eat it hastily, rinsing his mouth out afterward over the sink. Then, after grabbing his pannier and bike helmet from their peg by the front door, he would head off to the local community college where he'd taught introductory science and biology to freshmen for the last six years. Incoming nursing students mainly. To whom his classes were a practical necessity; to whom his passionate explications of membrane transport were just a way of getting into BIO309. They were certainly not moved to tears—as he sometimes was—by his re-enactments of cellular respiration, photosynthesis, alleles, polarities, and simple mutations.

There would, very occasionally, be a student within whom he detected a glimmer of light. Someone who exhibited more than the common classroom desire to appear "engaged"—to whom the subject matter at hand actually felt *real*. But these occasions were rare, and becoming rarer.

"It's extraordinary," he told his colleague Beth-Ann one day when their paths crossed, as they often did on Tuesday afternoons—when Beth-Ann was making her way from LB477 to LB323 and he was making his way from ML540 to LB475—"that here I am elucidating the very mysteries that allow them to exist at all, and they look right past me, this glassy look on their face, just hoping I'll give them an A."

But it was really no wonder it was so difficult for his students to focus on the mystery of life. They were too busy making eyes at the ceiling, flirting with the exposed rafters or with the slats between the broken blinds. They were too busy conducting electrical currents between themselves and everything else in the room: the pencils they twirled, the light that slanted in from the semi-opened blinds—even (though he barely noticed, and never would have acknowledged it) with Gil himself.

This was a limitation rather than an indication of any moral superiority on Gil's part. He was hardly aware of himself in front of women his own age these days, and it certainly didn't register with him that his broad-shouldered, slightly haggard look (chin beginning to sag, hair thinning) was not in itself unattractive. And that there was even something about him (a palpable disinterest in the fact of his own physical existence, perhaps—even as he instructed them on haploids and mitosis) that was, to nearly everyone who met him, at the very least, interesting.

In any case, it had been three weeks since Gil had announced to Alice, over dinner, that he was writing a novel.

Not really "announced"—that was too grand. "Suggested" was really more like it. Even though just hours before, the idea had more than "announced" itself to him; it had shot through him like a bolt of lightning. He would not merely "write" a novel, he'd thought as he rode his bike home after work one day in the pouring rain. He would *discover* it. He was a scientist, after all—not an artist. But science, Gil thought—as he merged from the campus bike path onto the main route—had for some time now been headed in the wrong direction. No, the secret of life was not—it occurred to him suddenly—in breaking things down into their component parts, but in seeing, instead, the way that everything existed together, in constant tension and relation, and yet at the same time analogously: the particular, for example, standing in for the whole, the whole for the part, and so on. It lay in seeing the way that everything repeated itself, existed in endless recombination, and yet at the same time was always unfamiliar, unknown, perpetually new.

Without realizing it, he put on his brakes—causing the rubber tire of his bike wheel to swerve and skid on the wet road. A car behind him swerved, too, blaring its horn—the driver glowering at him through a rain-streaked window.

It was as if Gil had confused his idea, as it had first occurred to him, with an actual physical direction he could move in. But the road continued to extend itself in only two directions. And the rain, too: it continued to pour down on him. Drenching him through a raincoat that had long ago outlived its waterproofing. Revelation or no, there was nowhere for Gil to go that he wasn't already going. And nothing for him to do except to stand there, sputtering; to blow rain off his top lip, taste snot, and shake his head in wonder and amazement at the way that everything had suddenly both fallen into place and stayed stubbornly the same.

By the time he got home and put the supper on, and a half-hour later or so Alice arrived, his enthusiasm for the idea had waned. Standing there in the rain, it had all seemed so natural, inevitable—his role in the whole thing effortlessly clear—but when he announced his intention to Alice over dinner—"I'm thinking about writing a novel"—it sounded more like a question than a firm resolve.

Alice had raised an eyebrow. If it wasn't for that, Gil would have assumed she hadn't heard. It was not at all uncommon between them these days that one or the other of them would just fail to hear.

Alice said, "Josephine, put the book down." (Gil realized only now that his daughter had been reading a book under the table.)

Josephine looked up suddenly, feigning shock. "What? Why? What's going on?"

"Your father's having a mid-life crisis," Alice said.

Josephine nodded and went back to her book.

"Is that what it's called?" Gil asked. He helped himself to more salad, scraping the wooden tongs along the bottom of the bowl. "Is that what this is?"

Alice rolled her eyes. But then she got up and ruffled his hair and kissed him on the top of his head. Their affections were like this now. Somewhere along the way, the line between how they behaved toward their children and one another had blurred. But to tell the truth, he didn't really mind. It was nice to have his hair ruffled, to be kissed on the top of his head. Who in their right mind would complain about that?

He knew that Alice was patronizing him, of course—but that was part of the pleasure. For both of them. Even when they were young, just starting out, it had been obvious that detecting some sort of weakness in Gil had caused Alice a small but noticeable surge of pleasure. She loved being able to give him that look— that single raised eyebrow. A look that confirmed for both of them that, whatever it was now, she had certainly seen coming.

Gil caught himself. He was being ungenerous, and quite honestly had no idea if any of the thoughts that had just occurred to him about himself and Alice were even true. He tried to scratch them from his mind—to actually delete them. There must be another explanation for her shift in mood. Like: why not, for example, that she loved him? That he still, after all these years, managed to please, and amuse, her? That she felt, if not passion for him, a genuine tenderness? Just as he did for her, most of the time.

Alice had been his first—his only.

POW! It had happened like that. Like the comic books he used to read. A simple splash of colour across the page. No— there had been no "before" to Alice. There had just been one frame, and then the next. It had been that clear, that out of his control. There had been just: Yes. And then again yes. The surety of physical action and reaction. So that if it was true what Mr. Einstein said—that gravitation cannot be held responsible for people falling in love—another system, more powerful than gravity, had been in charge. There was no other way of explaining the way that he had felt then—at twenty-three years old, on the last summer vacation he ever spent at home, when he first met Alice.

Everything before that time, he realized much later, not just his own measly existence but the whole world and everything in it, had, before Alice, been mere organic compound: inert, and lifeless, without either obvious meaning or form. Yes, it was only in the moment that (after dinner at the only restaurant in town that stayed open past eight o'clock) Alice had paused in the street, reached out, and taken Gil's hand that life had truly begun. This, he remembered thinking a moment later, as he leaned in and his lips touched hers, is the beginning; this is the first true thing.

But then four years later Josephine was born and life had begun all over again. He'd watched the crown of Josephine's head appear, and then—somewhere in the midst of the nurse's chatter and Alice's groans—he'd heard a new voice emerge, and had felt . . .

But it was impossible to describe because it was a feeling he'd never felt before, or since.

Except when, three years later, Felix was born, and life began, for the third time, all over again.

On the first day of his fourth week of writing, Gil drank four cups of coffee and gazed for two uninterrupted hours at his own thought process on the screen. Toward the end of the second hour, it occurred to him that the tremendous frustration he was feeling—as he strained against a limit he could not actually conceive—must have been precisely the frustration felt by primitive organisms, just before something shifted inside of them and they became the first forms of life.

Maybe this, he considered (as he created a new thought bubble on his screen and hurriedly typed the idea inside), was why human beings are still stuck in a veritable dark age of both empathy and reason, and have not been able to make any real advances for at least four thousand years. (PREHISTORY, Gil wrote underneath his previous thought.) They didn't know they had not yet evolved, and were still dependent on—and for the most part content within—the limits and stubborn inadequacies of their own pre-evolutionary forms. If he could just somehow manage to access again what he had, very briefly, riding home on his bike one exceedingly wet but otherwise ordinary afternoon . . . And then find some way to express whatever it was that he had discovered then: the way that (what was it?) everything happened tangentially and all at once . . .

(SIMULTANEITY, Gil wrote, then immediately deleted it.)

No, that wasn't it. That wasn't the word!

Gil's mind began to reel, his eyes burned. He opened a new file and, for the forty-five minutes remaining to him, stared nearly thoughtlessly at a blank screen, which—it is not an exaggeration to say—quite literally *glared* at him.

Inevitably, after a writing session such as this one, Gil would be distracted; would find himself inserting long digressions on the creative process in a classroom discussion of basic metabolic functions, for example, or reflecting whimsically on the role of metaphor in the middle of his introductory lecture, "The Evolution of Life."

On this particular afternoon—after having acknowledged,

for the first time, that he had absolutely no idea how to proceed with his novel, or why he had even begun—he found himself inexplicably inspired to suggest to his students that, when you got right down to it, *abiogenesis* was "just another word for love."

The air conditioner hummed. A few chairs squeaked. The more attractive students examined their wrists in the sunlight that streamed in through the broken blinds.

"Ab-i-o-genesis," Gil said again, hunting for a marker on the whiteboard ledge. "The process by which life arises from non-living matter, such as simple organic compounds. Is that not," he asked—giving up on the marker and turning back to the class—"also the definition of love?"

He had to watch it with this sort of thing, he knew that; and his teacher feedback forms agreed. His students all said things like, "I think I'd learn more if we could stick to the point," or "Much of the material covered was not actually on the exam." At the suggestion of his teaching mentor he had attempted to (her words) tone it down a little in the classroom—an effort that depressed him, and bored his students, but that had indeed led to better, or at least more consistent, evaluations, which (his tenure still pending) was what he needed right now.

At last, Gil found a marker, clicked off the top, and attempted to write the word on the board. The marker was dull, however, its tip frayed and nearly inkless, so he clicked the lid back in place and stepped over to the desk to hunt for another pen there. "Yes, if you are ever at a loss for the technical word . . ." Gil said as he shuffled around in the top drawer, "just remember . . ." A green marker came into view and he seized it, scrawled "Abiogenesis" in slanted green letters across the board.

"Yes, *love!*" he exclaimed as he turned to meet his students' alternately quizzical, amused, or disapproving stares. "It's not just a song from *Carnival!*, you know! It really does make the world go round."

He didn't exactly sing these last words, but the way he spoke them while bobbing his head slightly, implied—even to those students who had never heard of *Carnival!*—that they were intended to be sung.

Very shortly after that the minute hand collided with the hour hand at the top of the clock, and the students bolted from their seats. Gil found himself—still wielding the green whiteboard marker—facing an empty classroom, and feeling enormously depressed.

Well, it wasn't his fault, he thought, if life itself wasn't interesting. If even "love" could not be relied upon these days to catch a teenager's attention . . .

At one time, Gil thought—becoming angry—knowledge was something you had to actually *seek out*; something you had to work for, grasp after, struggle to uncover, and understand. At one time, "information" had not been enough, and there had been a sense, within the arts as well as the sciences, of things actually *mattering*.

For a few puzzling moments Gil felt so terrifically angry he wished a student would come wandering back into the room, as they sometimes did—having forgotten to ask for a grade revision, a letter of reference, or about an upcoming exam. He would have liked to really *have it out*. Wanted badly to confess; to complain; to argue a little—even come to blows. All quite ridiculous, of course, and (after the moment had passed, Gil excused himself) more like a nervous impulse than a proper desire.

Imagine. He—Gil—who had been the correct combination of likeable, mild, and willing to compromise all his life so that he had never gotten into a serious conflict with anyone. Not even with Alice. Even when things had been rough—as they certainly had been sometimes.

As they were right now.

Yes, Gil admitted. That is exactly what you would call it. What he and Alice were going through. A "rough patch." And yet—he had nothing to show for it. No bruises, not even really of the spirit. Just the inevitable steady wear, impossible to insure against. Yes, they were both worn out, that was obvious. But there wasn't, and never had been, any real break—and it was entirely possible that nothing was even wrong at all. That Alice, who had never been anything but supportive—a model mother, a perfect wife— had nothing to do with it. That Gil himself was the rough patch; that he had only himself to blame. And that the sudden disgust he had felt a moment ago for an entire generation had been merely a sad, middle-aged attempt at excusing himself and his own inadequacies—as a teacher, a father, a husband, a would-be novelist, and a human being. Bemoaning the systemic apathies of Late Capitalism and the demise of knowledge was, after all, a whole lot easier than amending his approach to parenting, partnership, or classroom teaching. Perhaps, Gil thought, "the yawning void" (his current favourite nickname for the Westmoreland College student body he faced every day) had become more literal than he'd supposed, and he was—as Alice had rather tolerantly put it the other day over breakfast—beginning to crack up a bit.

Gil moved to the window and twisted the curtain rod so that the slats on the blinds closed with a snap. He picked up his pannier and his helmet and glanced quickly about to make sure he hadn't forgotten anything. He stepped out into the hall and closed the door firmly behind him. What happened next is difficult to describe, because it happened for only a few brief moments and—the result of a minor hallucination—only in Gil's mind.

Upon exiting the classroom Gil turned left, as usual, toward the set of double doors that opened onto the quad, but instead of the (at a rough guess) no more than fifty feet between himself and the doors, the hall stretched out nearly endlessly. The double doors—which he could just barely make out in the distance—appeared, rather than to mark any end, to suggest the beginning of still vaster and less traversable distances.

Gil's heart began to pound, then to flutter irregularly.

Was he having a heart attack?

He had heard that people who had them tended to complain, not of pain, exactly, but of feeling disoriented, not quite themselves . . .

Gil was certainly feeling both of these things now. Even the question "Was he having a heart attack?" seemed to have very little to do with his own life. It was as though he was reading the question aloud from the pages of *Plant and Animal Physiology*—the standard textbook he assigned to his introductory classes. As though it came complete with various sub-questions and categories for discussion, all of which then began to occur to him sequentially, and in the following order: A) Was it possible to die like this, in the middle of the hall, and for no apparent reason other than being unable to see a more or less literal "way out"? B) If it *was* possible, and Gil really was about to die, had his final words really been an unsung phrase from *Carnival!*—the actual tune of which he had never properly known? C) If he was not about to die, as now (his heart beginning to pound more regularly) seemed more probable, was thinking he was going to die—and this experience, whatever it was—standing in for death in a way that, if he could find a way to pay attention, he might parse? What did it mean on a personal level—in other words, Gil wondered—to walk into a hall one day and see only infinite space stretching around you, on every side?

It meant (he understood suddenly) that he had become a known quantity—a finite figure in the tremendous, unthinkable, and ultimately unbalanced equation that was his own life.

Where, that is, as a child he had extended indefinitely, all the way out to the farthest elliptical edge of the universe, and even as a young man had never been able to clearly distinguish between himself and everything that existed beyond, he had, in middle age, begun to exist simply as himself. A simple line segment, a ray—extending between two known, or at least easily foreseeable, points.

Gil shook his head to clear it. The hallway tilted and then righted itself. He looked left toward the double doors. Then right. Then left again. As though there really was more than one way to go.

When there wasn't. Only the doors to his left led outside to the quad, where he had locked his bike to a post earlier that day.

He had no other choice but to move in that direction. To open the door, retrieve the bike, and make his way across the quad. He had no other choice but to hang a left at the end of the street and head across the park toward home.

It was a short ride—fifteen minutes at most. The kids would be home already, having let themselves in. Alice would be on her way. He could almost guarantee that any moment his pocket would buzz and it would be a text from her saying she was stuck in traffic and would he put the dinner on? That pretty soon he would be standing in the kitchen gazing into the white light of the refrigerator wondering what he might possibly retrieve from its depths.

He'd yell "Stir-fry or fish?" to the kids, who would, by then, be lounging on the couch in the other room, waiting impatiently for their hour of screen time. It was possible that one or both of them might look up and frown at whatever he said. And it was possible that, as they did so, it would occur to him how strange and unfamiliar his children were to him these days. It would almost break Gil's heart to realize, in that moment, that his children—his perfect children, who had been delivered into the world as all children are, by a miracle—were beginning to enter the semi-dormant stage of adolescence. That he was going to have to take it on simple faith for a little while that it would all begin again, somehow . . .

One simply had to choose, Gil told himself, as he began—at first unsteadily—down the hall. That was all there was to it. How could you write a novel if you couldn't, in the first place, simply choose a story—then write it down?

So what, he thought as he stepped under the red glow of the

Exit sign, if in writing it, it became "just another story"? If he did not, in the end, discover a new form of life, but just another way of describing the one that he had?

That (he instructed himself as he pushed open a heavy door and was hit by a sudden draft of late-September air) was all that he was capable of, and therefore (he realized as he unlocked his bicycle, attached his pannier to the rack, and fastened his helmet under his chin) was all that he wanted. To have his story—whatever it was, or was going to be—be just another story among all possible stories.

Pedalling home, he repeated this resolution to himself several times, until the phrase began to run through his mind almost mechanically. Until the words, and their rhythms, became like the movements of his muscles as he pedalled downhill. Or (because he didn't need to exert himself very much at all in the last five to ten minutes of the ride) of the pedals themselves. Until he didn't have to think of them at all, and instead they, like his body, were propelled only by gravity, by a simple inertia, and—his mind utterly blank—he was filled only with the supreme desire that he would not die. That death was not, after all, and as it so far appeared, inevitable.

For the first time since he was a child, Gil prayed.

He knew it was preposterous. That to ask for, to expect, the universe to answer to his own, very particular, needs and desires was unreasonable at best—but that is what he did. He pedalled slowly, mechanically, without resistance, downhill, and he prayed for the preservation and safekeeping of himself and of his wife, Alice, whom he had once loved so much that the entire world had, it would be only a small exaggeration to say, shifted, and for his children; and then—to ease his conscience, and because, very briefly, he did not understand the difference—for all living creatures on earth.

THE REMEMBERER

THE ARCHIVE WAS INDEFENSIBLE and security breaches were at an all-time high when a girl (six years old, and in every other respect quite ordinary—living with her extended family somewhere in the banlieues) was discovered with what could only be described as a virtually limitless power of recall. With two hundred thousand years of accumulated knowledge at stake, there seemed no better solution than to rely, once again, upon the faculties of the human mind.

Of course, they had to admit from the outset the idea was flawed. That it was, at best, a "temporary measure." But it was generally agreed—even by those scientists, historians, administrators, and policy makers who (all bent on arriving, respectively, at a more sustainable solution) did not generally agree upon anything—that if properly educated, this remarkable young girl might buy them all a little valuable time.

A rigorous and fully funded education program was quickly provided by the state, employing a team of researchers from every imaginable field. The Masters, as the team of thirty-seven came to be known, instructed the girl in every stage of the development of human thought, covering every topic, every method, every (often conflicting) angle and approach to science, art, technology, trade, and history itself over the past two hundred thousand years. The girl's appetite for knowledge proved so voracious that by the time she was nine years old her "memory" extended back to the beginnings of human life on earth. By eleven, she could remember rising from the mud; by twelve—with a reflexive shudder—the moment the first unicellular structure divided into two; by fourteen (and in not only accurate but moving detail) she could describe the conflicting pressures of gravity and time that caused the earth to strain and shift, that set the continents adrift and gave birth to mountain ranges, ocean beds, polar ice, and magnetic fields.

The fact that the girl was—aside from her extraordinary memory—really quite ordinary was not at first considered a disadvantage. She'd been removed from her extended family shortly after her genius was discovered—her only influences the thirty-seven Masters since the age of six—but she continued to demonstrate the usual range of human emotion, both delighting and confounding her Masters with bursts of frank affection, unreasonable anger, and unexplained joy.

The program had been named Whirlwind III, after the first real-time computer system to benefit from the invention of core memory, but not only (the Masters boasted) did the girl already possess more core memory than any computer operating system that had been designed, she was also adaptable, fiercely loyal, and unusually empathetic—three things that had so far eluded every other system of record-keeping, including the most advanced forms of AI.

As the girl grew older, however, her passions became less predictable, as well as less easy to temper. During an especially volatile moment at age fourteen, she even threatened to end her own life. ("What do I care?" she'd shrieked at the Masters. "They're *your* memories—not mine!") The Masters did what they could to hush up the incident, but, inevitably, word got out—and the backlash was fierce. Until this point, the program had received wide and popular support; millions had happily followed the education and development of the bright-eyed, red-cheeked "Rememberer" in the tabloids and the weekly news. But now nearly everyone began to complain. It was obvious, many early critics of the program warned, that the burden of two hundred thousand years of accumulated knowl-edge was too much for any human being. It was inhumane—another especially vocal group argued—to invest the full range of human experience in a single child precisely because it pre-vented her from actually participating in the full range of human experience. No wonder the girl was increasingly troubled by insomnia, and alternated between fits of rage and despair! No wonder she had threatened to end her own life—and with it every possibility of establishing a more permanent record! No wonder that, shortly after, at the age of sixteen, she began to suffer inexplicable flashes of "darkness"! (Petit mal seizures, the neurologists called them, but upon further examination, no physical or biochemical cause could be found for the episodes, and it was concluded that nothing was wrong.)

The Masters fought among themselves, each one blaming another for the girl's emotional volatility and her "absences," which (despite the doctors' diagnosis) continued with increas-ing frequency. Each time they occurred—without explanation or warning—the girl would be unable to speak, and for several terrifying seconds her face would go blank. Each time, two hundred thousand years of accumulated knowledge would flash horribly before the Masters' eyes.

And it was no wonder. Ten years had passed since the program began, but still those (scientists, historians, administrators, and policy makers alike) dedicated to arriving at a more permanent solution were no closer to finding one. The girl remained their only hope . . . and yet the situation was hopeless. The public still spoke out from time to time, but as they began to lose interest, it was the girl herself who became the program's toughest critic, describing its limitations as insurmountable and systemic—uniquely tied to the limits and vagaries not only of her education but also of her own mind.

What should trouble them most, she protested, was that she was unable to pinpoint where one memory left off from another—or where they began. Rather than a continuous, chronological archive, her memories were instead fragmented, scattered, often vague. That they would surface strangely, like photographs in a chemical bath—transformed into negative images of themselves. But that rather than—like a photograph—indexing any actual experience, they seemed instead to mark a void.

And what (she demanded one day—chin jutted, eyes sharp and hard; the very picture of adolescent impudence) of memories that could not be indexed at all? That were instead mere whiffs of sensations, brief bursts of colour, a feeling of being pricked by something—of going under, as beneath a sudden wave? What in fact were those memories, or any others (in which, say, she scoured the depths of the first oceans, or awakened in the mind of a cephalopod as the simple contrast between darkness and light), if not the products of someone else's imagination? What she "remembered" was in any case not knowledge. It was speculation, conjecture. The purest of fictions!

In other moods, she would grumble that she hardly saw the point. The history of human thought, she would sigh despairingly, was nothing more, after all, than an arduous dream. In still other moods, she would become fierce, aloof. Only to brighten a moment later, laugh out loud, or surprise someone with a firm embrace.

Emotional turbulence was, of course (the Masters reasoned), an unavoidable side effect to the girl's demanding course of study. What else could they expect from a young woman capable of grasping—simultaneously—both Cantor's continuum hypothesis and mathematical Platonism? Or of recalling, in excruciating detail, what it felt like to die in battle both as a proud defender of the Orange Free State and as a Basotho child? It was for this reason, after all, that the human mind had evolved to remember only selectively. For this reason that experience became symbolic, then relative; that memories receded—sometimes altogether disappeared. Forgetting was as simple a defence mechanism as sex, or flight, the evolution of which (as the girl concurred) could be traced back to the very origin of the species.

It is not, perhaps, so surprising, then, that as the years continued to pass, and the question (how best to preserve two hundred thousand years of accumulated knowledge?) remained unanswered, it also became less pressing. Enthusiasm for the program had long since waned, funding was siphoned to more immediate projects and concerns, and the girl continued to suffer from interruptive flashes of darkness. A general despondency and a sense of collective defeat settled over the twenty-two remaining Masters—though some optimistically maintained that the "flashes" marked not a limit but an as-yet-unexplored direction for the program. They implored the girl to describe, as minutely as possible, these periods of "absolute darkness," hoping she might offer some clue as to what was on "the other side."

She always left them disappointed.

The problem, she explained, was that she could never quite recall the darkness as it actually occurred, but only in relation to *what happened next* . . .

The less optimistic Masters coughed, or shifted uncomfortably in their seats. For some time now, it had been gallingly difficult for the girl to recall anything abstract—especially anything of a precognitive nature—without falling back on the bad habit of metaphor. She had also become increasingly prone to either conflating events or recalling only their general themes. And it was irritating even to the optimists among them that she insisted on relating everything from the first person limited, as if the whole of human history had actually happened to *her*.

Inevitably, whenever these shortcomings were discussed, one of the Masters would—in a wry voice that was deliberately impossible to read—remind them all that Whirlwind III had never, after all, been anything but a temporary solution.

"Yes," another would reply dolefully. "And since we're no closer to a better one, perhaps it's time to start with a clean slate."

"And do away with two hundred thousand years of accumulated human knowledge?" another would gasp. "Even *accepting*
that the record has undergone, in the last few years—ahem—a
slight process of revision, it hardly seems like a decision one
could *reasonably* make."

"We've simply invested too much time and money into this
program to pull out now," another would assert. And that
would be the end of it—at least for a while.

One day, a philologist spoke up. She was among the more timid
of the group, and had rarely contributed to the debate.

"It may be," she said, "that we are overlooking a basic fact."

Everyone turned, surprised, and looked at the philologist.

"And what is that?" demanded an attorney at law.

Ignoring the question, and avoiding looking the attorney
in the eye, the philologist continued. "Just because," she said,
"the subject of our study has so far been compelled to fall back
on metaphor does not mean, at least necessarily, that the mem
ories themselves actually exist that way. Language, after all, is
designed not to either imitate or replace, but instead to *represent*
the objects of our experience. It's a complicated code—purposely
indirect. Intended to suggest *affinity* rather than to reproduce
substantial structure."

"Are you suggesting," a philosopher asked cautiously, "that
the subject is merely a veiled reference to the object?"

"That she exists only as a sort of cipher," a cryptanalyst put in
excitedly, "which, if properly decoded, could point us toward the
unbiased historical record, which—as you seem to be suggesting,

and despite our inevitable biases—beneath it all, actually exists? That it is just a matter of getting beyond language, to what the language was designed to simultaneously obscure and convey?"

In a voice that suggested the conversation had strayed, a psychoanalyst turned to the subject herself who (though forgotten) had been present all along, and asked her to recount to them her earliest memory.

A statistician groaned. "And what will that prove?"

"Shh!" a poet replied.

A deafening silence ensued, and after several minutes had ticked slowly by, even the optimists began to assume that the girl was suffering from another petit mal. Either that or she simply had nothing to say.

But then—so quietly that some of the Masters failed to hear—the girl said a single word: "Imagine." And then nothing more for such a long time that even those who had heard began to suspect that they hadn't.

"Imagine," the girl said again. "Imagine you are looking at a painting of a landscape and suddenly you are not yourself at all, looking at the painting of the landscape, but you are the landscape itself. Or the small glint of light, for example, on the waves in the far corner of the landscape's frame."

As she spoke, her voice began to gain confidence, then speed. "Imagine being just that," she said. "Just the brushstroke—without thought to the brush, or the hand."

When she had finished speaking—and though they had come no closer to a solution, and nothing at all had been "proven"— the Masters were forced to admit, once again, that despite the girl's episodes, an incurable dependence on metaphor, and a tendency to lapse (as then) into near-uninterpretable lyricism, her capacity for retaining—and sometimes expressing—the breadth and complexity of human experience remained nothing short of extraordinary.

"And that alone," remarked a physicist, by way of closing, "is a reason to continue the program. One does not, after all, pursue science, or any other worthwhile human endeavour, with anything like a guarantee. One pursues it only with the sense—a sense that all of us have had, at one point or another, here—that one has touched upon the extraordinary."

Despite—or because of—the Masters' continued, if faltering, faith, the girl was increasingly plagued by flashes of darkness and fits of dread. She imagined being subjected, at an undesignated point in the future and by an unknown adversary, to some terrible inquisition—and wondered how much, after so many years of silence, she would be willing to withhold

She was visited by nightmares, hardly slept; her health suffered terribly. Once again the physicians were called, and once again they reported that the girl was in perfect health, that nothing was wrong. In the end, she diagnosed her condition herself: "the return of the repressed."

If she only had some outlet, she sobbed, some way of relating her experiences . . . creatively, perhaps! Yes! Perhaps that was the answer! She could translate her experiences—everything she had felt and learned—into something else altogether. She could invent a whole other language if necessary, so that (though perhaps recognizable in certain parts) whatever it was she ultimately managed to express would be utterly transformed, virtually impossible to trace . . .

The Masters shook their heads.

But could they even imagine? the girl cried. Had they no empathy at all?

"Think of it!" she begged. "Two hundred thousand years of accumulated knowledge, and no one to talk to—no one who even tries to understand! It's enough to drive one positively mad."

But regulations had only tightened since the project began, and the creative arts (as the Masters soon informed the girl) had always been particularly inconvenient for exactly the reason to which she herself referred. It was impossible to regulate. There was simply no way of anticipating if—or in what way—its meaning might one day be interpreted.

It was not long after this that the girl did go mad. At least, this was the only explanation offered by even the most optimistic Masters for why—instead of darkness, or faded picture-postcard memories of the past—the future began to flare up suddenly before her, in hallucinatory flashes.

At first, she had trouble differentiating these bewildering new episodes from the others, but she soon began to notice that where even her most abstract memories always appeared in the guise of some external image, or object, and she could only ever experience "absolute darkness" in terms of what it was not, the future was generated from somewhere inside her, existed only in positive terms, and was hers alone.

And yet, despite the thrill of freedom she felt at encountering—for the first time in living memory—what lay beyond living memory, the first thing the girl foresaw was her own annihilation.

"There will come a time," she announced to the Masters one afternoon, "that, for the precise reason that you once honoured and celebrated my tremendous gift, you will turn against me.

"Even now," she warned, "I have already become too dangerous for you, and my memories—rather than a resource or a point of pride—have become a risk, a liability. Even I cannot tell you what, if captured, I would or would not say. I am, after all, only flesh and blood—no more resistant to abuse or simple boredom than any one of you.

"Who knows what little it might take to make me speak? As you know, I have complained often of my own great loneliness—my urge to unburden myself of all that I know.

"This will occur to you," said the girl, sadly. "It is occurring to you now. Very soon, the risk will strike you as simply too great for the sake of the simple past. There is, after all, you will think, the future to consider.

"And this is it. Before our adversaries have the opportunity to do so, it is you who will destroy me. You will end what you began, having come no nearer to your goal. And I cannot blame you.

"Because, when I think back to everything that has happened, to all the decisions I made, or failed to make; to the wars I helped to win or lose; to the thousands of children I bore; to the mistakes I made, the lovers I lost, or, against my better judgment, kept; to the ideas I had and discarded; to the faith that was born, then lost, then born again, on so many different occasions, and in so many ways . . .

"When I remember what it felt to be a simple splash of light on a painting of a landscape I have never seen—to be just that simple contrast between darkness and light—to be the product of every imagination, and every hand . . .

"When I remember what it felt like to be just an empty waiting thing, when there was nothing to wait for, nothing yet to begin . . . I cannot blame you. Because at every moment there is only one decision, and that is the decision made by every moment—in deepest ignorance—as it returns to what it has not yet been.

"You will make this decision, just as you have made every other: in perfect darkness. Because that is the future—which I have seen and foretold."

The Masters bowed their heads. They felt embarrassed for themselves, and for the girl—and then ashamed. Because somehow they all felt certain that what she said was true.

Finally, the oldest among them cleared her throat. "If you are right," the old Master said, "and the future is, by contrast to the present or the past, of our own making, why choose to speak of your own demise? I cannot help but be reminded of the old tale—I forget where I heard it now—the tale of the bridge across which you were permitted to pass only if you told the guard in advance where you were going and why, and swore on oath that whatever you said was true. If you swore the truth, you were permitted to pass, but if you swore falsely, you would die on the gallows. There was no chance of pardon.

"One day, a young man came along who swore an oath before crossing the bridge that he would die on the gallows. His oath perplexed the judge and jury, because they knew that if the man was allowed to pass freely, then he would have lied—and so, according to law, must die. But if they hanged him, he would have been telling the truth—and so, according to the law, he must be set free."

"I am afraid," said another of the Masters, rising and glancing nervously about—including in the direction of the girl, though she did not appear to be listening—"that this long story is not at all to the point."

"On the contrary," the old Master said. "Is it not possible that we are faced, once again, with the decision whether or not to bind ourselves to truth by death or to pass by lies? As well as with the questions, which path is more honest in the end? And by whom, or by what, are we judged?"

ACKNOWLEDGMENTS

"The Opening" first appeared in "Short Story Sunday," on November 30, 2014.

"A Horse, a Vine" first appeared in *XO Orpheus: Fifty New Myths* (Penguin 2013), edited by Kate Bernheimer. I am grateful to Kate for selecting this story, as well as for her thoughtful editorial suggestions. I am also grateful to myholysmoke.com for the original inspiration for this story—and for the wording of the advertisement Dean reads on pages 131 and 132.

"The Rememberer" first appeared in *Granta* 141: Canada. I am grateful to Madeleine Thien and Catherine Leroux for selecting this story, and to Maddie for her careful reading and comments.

Thank you to Sam Ace and Rebecca Silver Slayter for their helpful insights and suggestions for "Mr. Doyle's Ancestral Genetic Homeland."

Thank you to my agent, Tracy Bohan, for her continued belief in, and support of, my work.

And to my wonderful editor, Nicole Winstanley, for her energy, editorial insights, and friendship.

Thank you, also, to my husband, John Melillo, for his love and encouragement—as well as for listening to, and helping me to revise, countless drafts of these stories.

And—as always—thank you to Janet Shively, my mother.